Walt Disney's Donald Duck

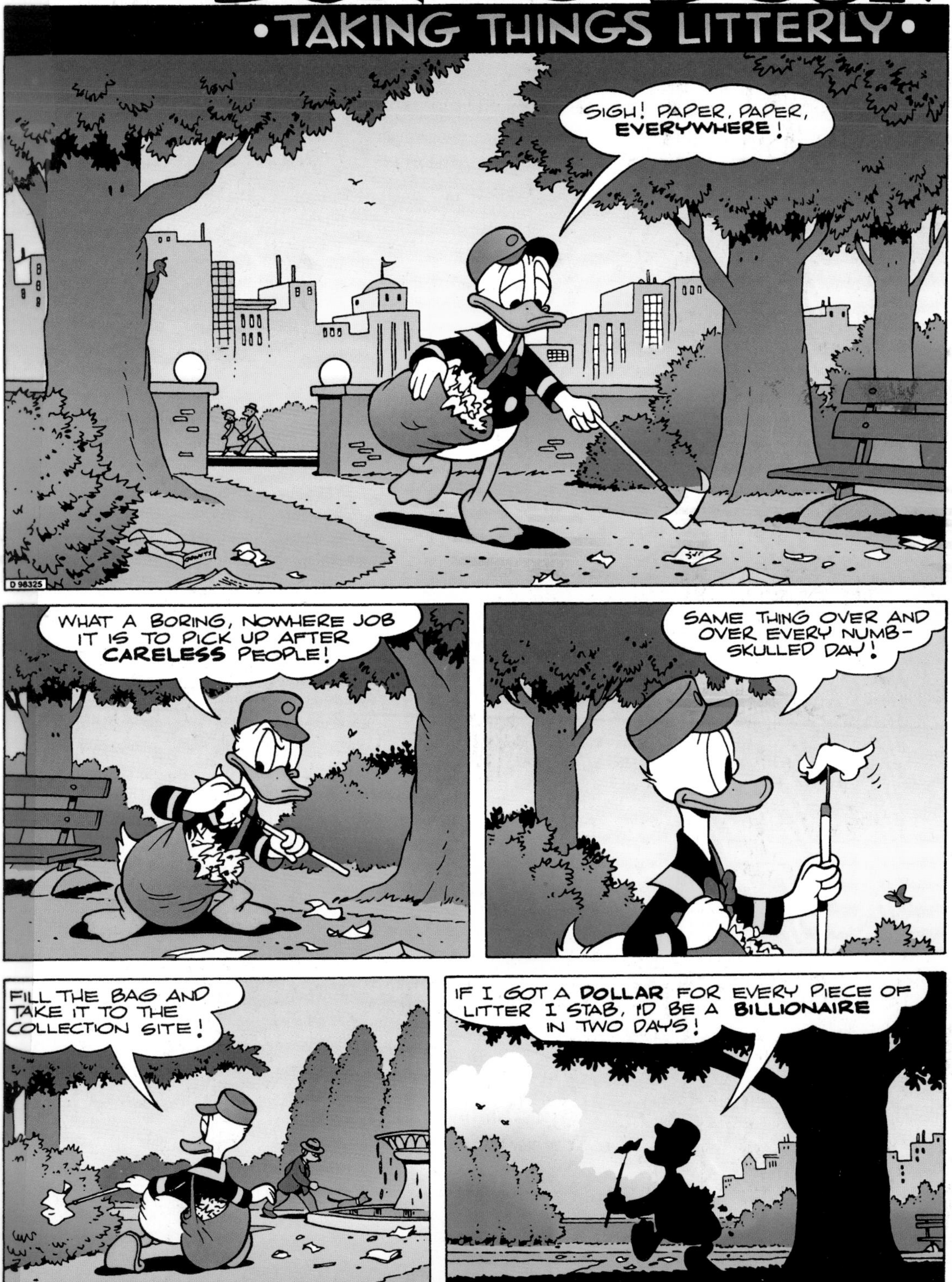
•TAKING THINGS LITTERLY•
SIGH! PAPER, PAPER, EVERYWHERE!
D 98325
WHAT A BORING, NOWHERE JOB IT IS TO PICK UP AFTER CARELESS PEOPLE!
SAME THING OVER AND OVER EVERY NUMB-SKULLED DAY!
FILL THE BAG AND TAKE IT TO THE COLLECTION SITE!
IF I GOT A DOLLAR FOR EVERY PIECE OF LITTER I STAB, I'D BE A BILLIONAIRE IN TWO DAYS!

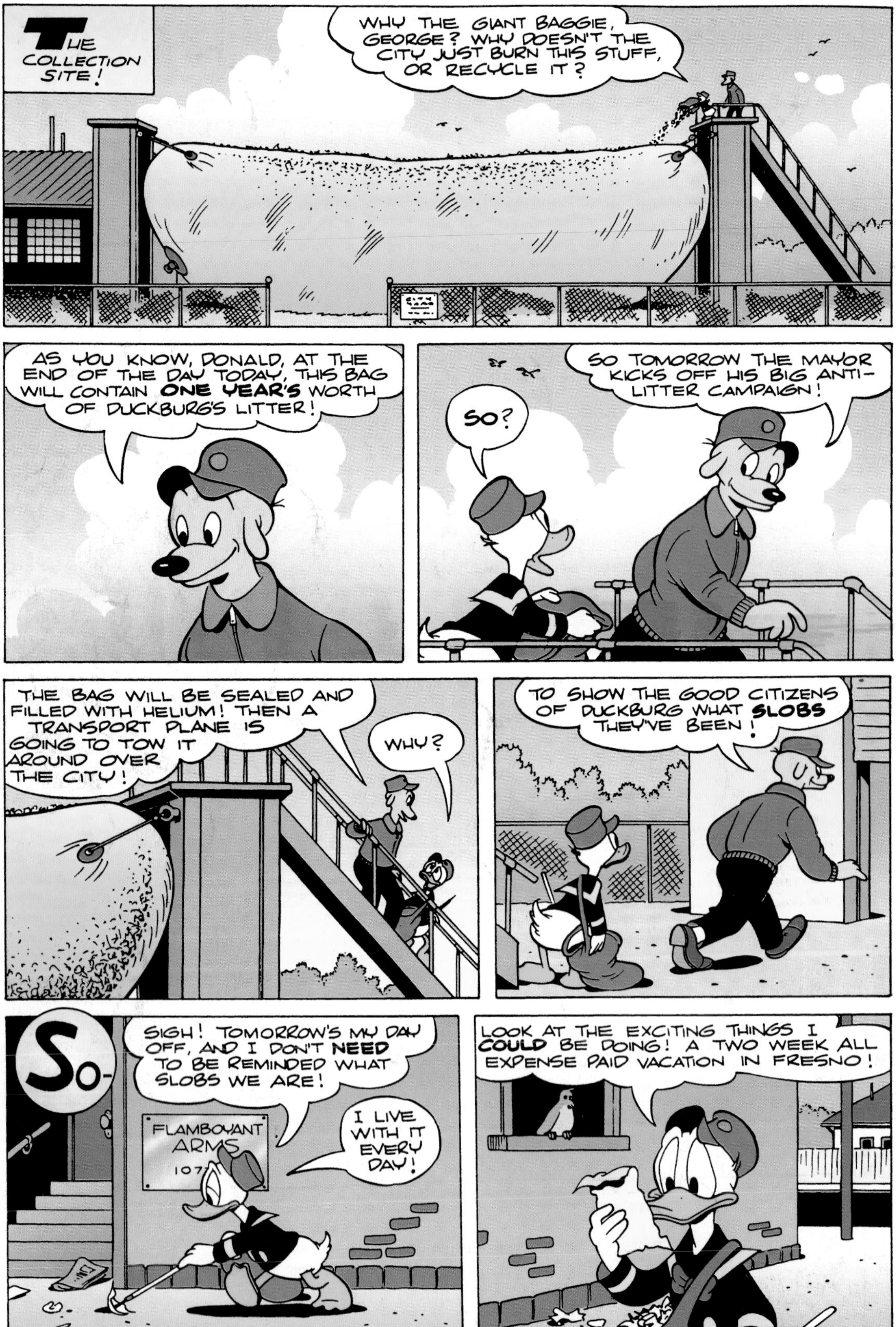
THE COLLECTION SITE!
WHY THE GIANT BAGGIE, GEORGE? WHY DOESN'T THE CITY JUST BURN THIS STUFF, OR RECYCLE IT?
AS YOU KNOW, DONALD, AT THE END OF THE DAY TODAY, THIS BAG WILL CONTAIN ONE YEAR'S WORTH OF DUCKBURG'S LITTER!
SO?
SO TOMORROW THE MAYOR KICKS OFF HIS BIG ANTI-LITTER CAMPAIGN!
THE BAG WILL BE SEALED AND FILLED WITH HELIUM! THEN A TRANSPORT PLANE IS GOING TO TOW IT AROUND OVER THE CITY!
WHY?
TO SHOW THE GOOD CITIZENS OF DUCKBURG WHAT SLOBS THEY'VE BEEN!
SO-
SIGH! TOMORROW'S MY DAY OFF, AND I DON'T NEED TO BE REMINDED WHAT SLOBS WE ARE!
FLAMBOYANT ARMS
I LIVE WITH IT EVERY DAY!
LOOK AT THE EXCITING THINGS I COULD BE DOING! A TWO WEEK ALL EXPENSE PAID VACATION IN FRESNO!

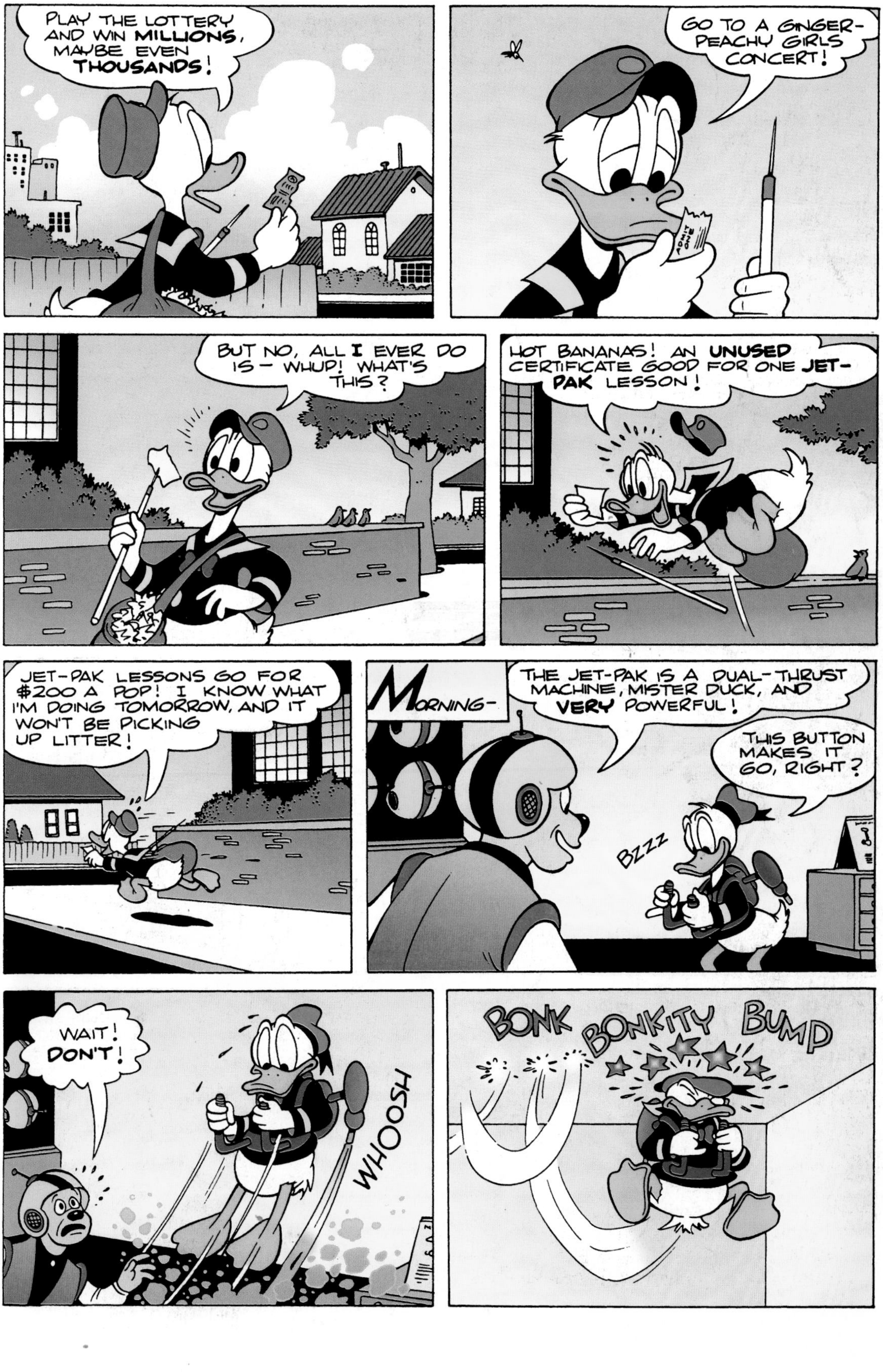
PLAY THE LOTTERY AND WIN **MILLIONS**, MAYBE EVEN **THOUSANDS**!
GO TO A GINGER-PEACHY GIRLS CONCERT!
ADMIT ONE
BUT NO, ALL **I** EVER DO IS— WHUP! WHAT'S THIS?
HOT BANANAS! AN **UNUSED** CERTIFICATE GOOD FOR ONE **JET-PAK** LESSON!
JET-PAK LESSONS GO FOR $200 A POP! I KNOW WHAT I'M DOING TOMORROW, AND IT WON'T BE PICKING UP LITTER!
MORNING-
THE JET-PAK IS A DUAL-THRUST MACHINE, MISTER DUCK, AND **VERY** POWERFUL!
THIS BUTTON MAKES IT GO, RIGHT?
BZZZ
WAIT! **DON'T**!
WHOOSH
BONK BONKITY BUMP

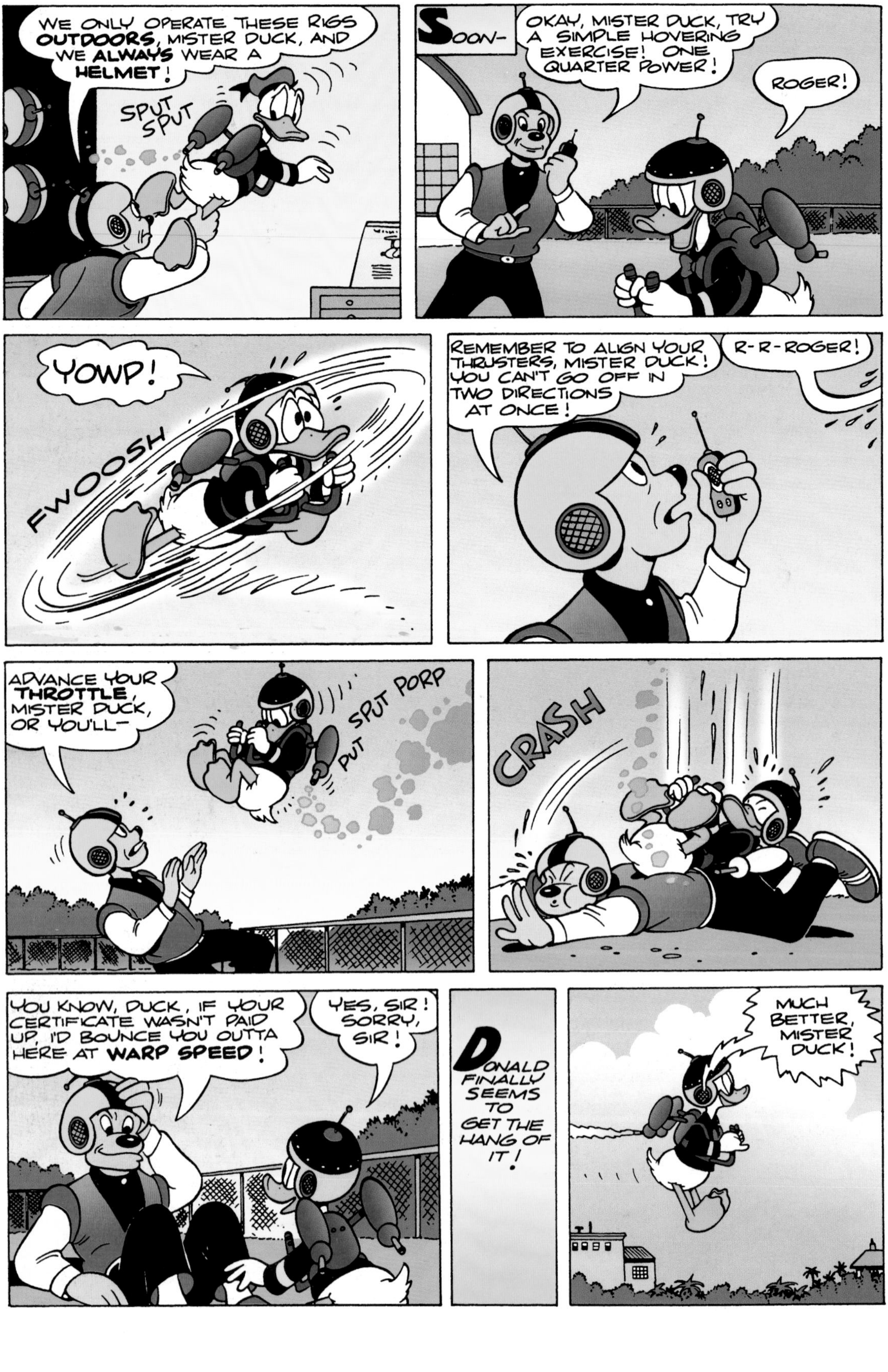
WE ONLY OPERATE THESE RIGS **OUTDOORS**, MISTER DUCK, AND WE **ALWAYS** WEAR A **HELMET**!
SPUT SPUT
SOON-
OKAY, MISTER DUCK, TRY A SIMPLE HOVERING EXERCISE! ONE QUARTER POWER!
ROGER!
YOWP!
FWOOSH
REMEMBER TO ALIGN YOUR THRUSTERS, MISTER DUCK! YOU CAN'T GO OFF IN TWO DIRECTIONS AT ONCE!
R-R-ROGER!
ADVANCE YOUR **THROTTLE**, MISTER DUCK, OR YOU'LL—
SPUT PORP
PUT
CRASH
YOU KNOW, DUCK, IF YOUR CERTIFICATE WASN'T PAID UP, I'D BOUNCE YOU OUTTA HERE AT **WARP SPEED**!
YES, SIR! SORRY, SIR!
DONALD FINALLY SEEMS TO GET THE HANG OF IT!
MUCH BETTER, MISTER DUCK!

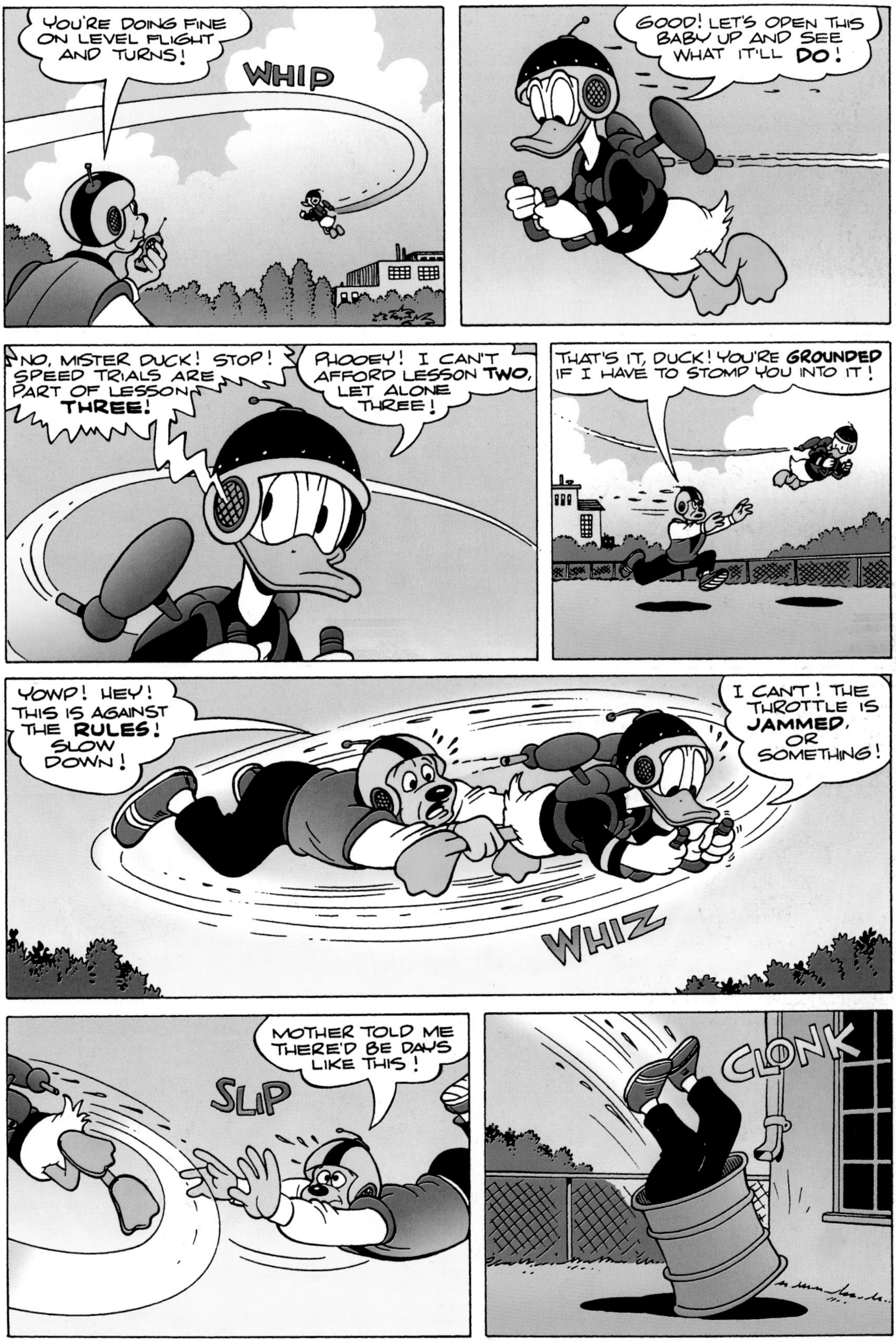
YOU'RE DOING FINE ON LEVEL FLIGHT AND TURNS!
WHIP
GOOD! LET'S OPEN THIS BABY UP AND SEE WHAT IT'LL DO!
NO, MISTER DUCK! STOP! SPEED TRIALS ARE PART OF LESSON THREE!
PHOOEY! I CAN'T AFFORD LESSON TWO, LET ALONE THREE!
THAT'S IT, DUCK! YOU'RE GROUNDED IF I HAVE TO STOMP YOU INTO IT!
YOWP! HEY! THIS IS AGAINST THE RULES! SLOW DOWN!
I CAN'T! THE THROTTLE IS JAMMED, OR SOMETHING!
WHIZ
MOTHER TOLD ME THERE'D BE DAYS LIKE THIS!
SLIP
CLONK

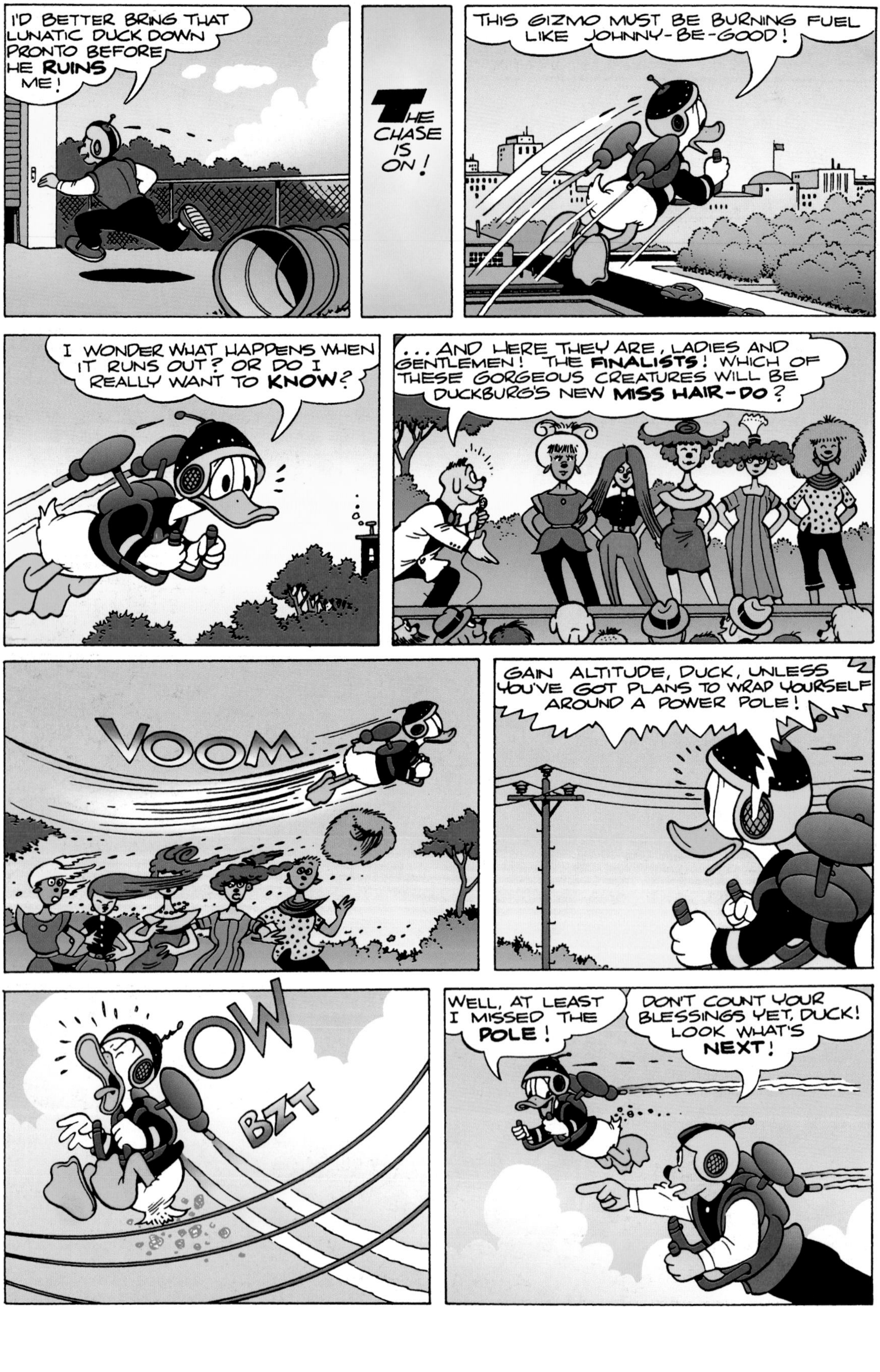
I'D BETTER BRING THAT LUNATIC DUCK DOWN PRONTO BEFORE HE **RUINS** ME!
THE CHASE IS ON!
THIS GIZMO MUST BE BURNING FUEL LIKE JOHNNY-BE-GOOD!
I WONDER WHAT HAPPENS WHEN IT RUNS OUT? OR DO I REALLY WANT TO **KNOW**?
...AND HERE THEY ARE, LADIES AND GENTLEMEN! THE **FINALISTS**! WHICH OF THESE GORGEOUS CREATURES WILL BE DUCKBURG'S NEW **MISS HAIR-DO**?
VOOM
GAIN ALTITUDE, DUCK, UNLESS YOU'VE GOT PLANS TO WRAP YOURSELF AROUND A POWER POLE!
OW
BZT
WELL, AT LEAST I MISSED THE **POLE**!
DON'T COUNT YOUR BLESSINGS YET, DUCK! LOOK WHAT'S **NEXT**!

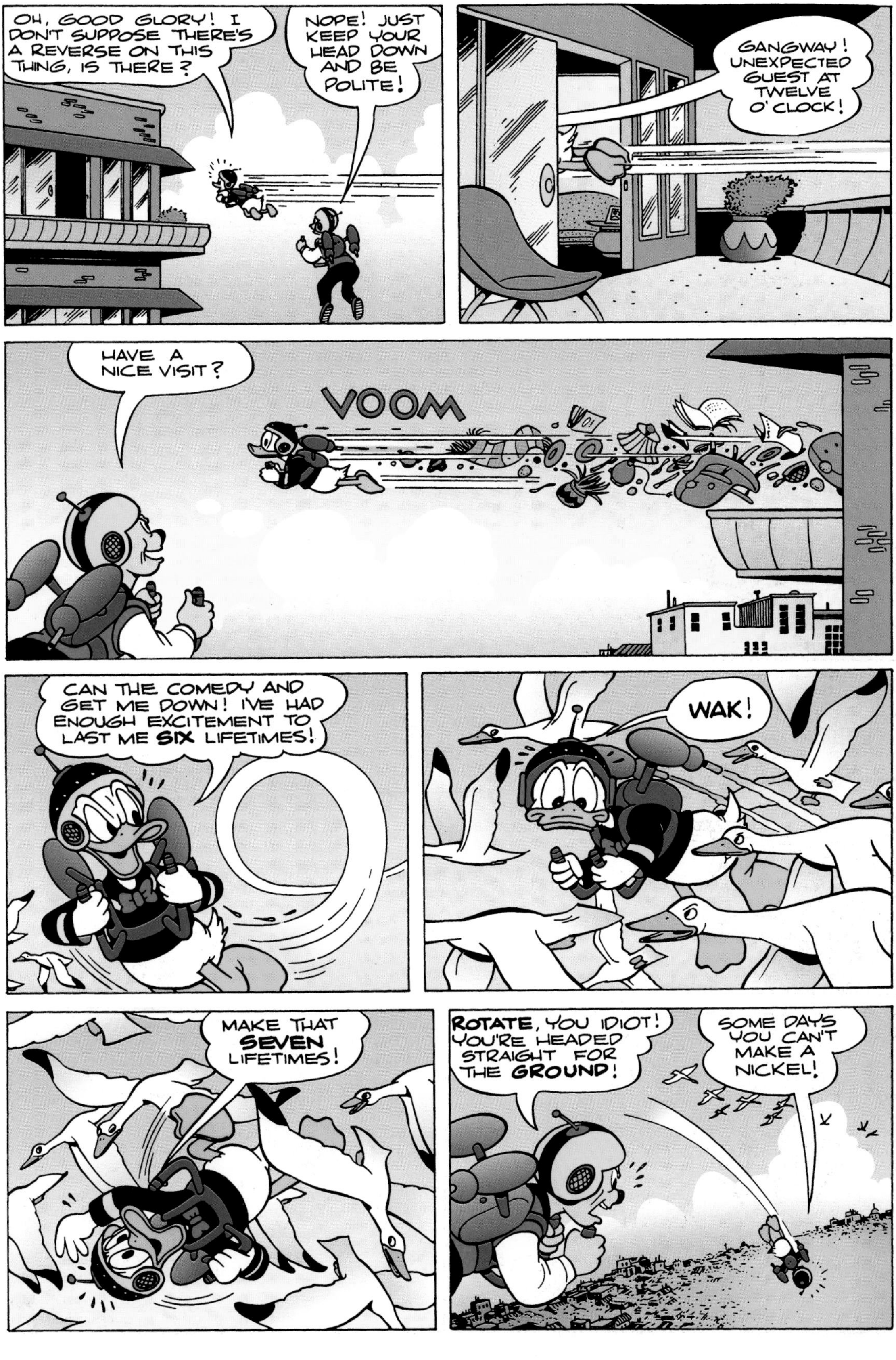

OH, GOOD GLORY! I DON'T SUPPOSE THERE'S A REVERSE ON THIS THING, IS THERE?
NOPE! JUST KEEP YOUR HEAD DOWN AND BE POLITE!
GANGWAY! UNEXPECTED GUEST AT TWELVE O' CLOCK!
HAVE A NICE VISIT?
VOOM
CAN THE COMEDY AND GET ME DOWN! I'VE HAD ENOUGH EXCITEMENT TO LAST ME SIX LIFETIMES!
WAK!
MAKE THAT SEVEN LIFETIMES!
ROTATE, YOU IDIOT! YOU'RE HEADED STRAIGHT FOR THE GROUND!
SOME DAYS YOU CAN'T MAKE A NICKEL!

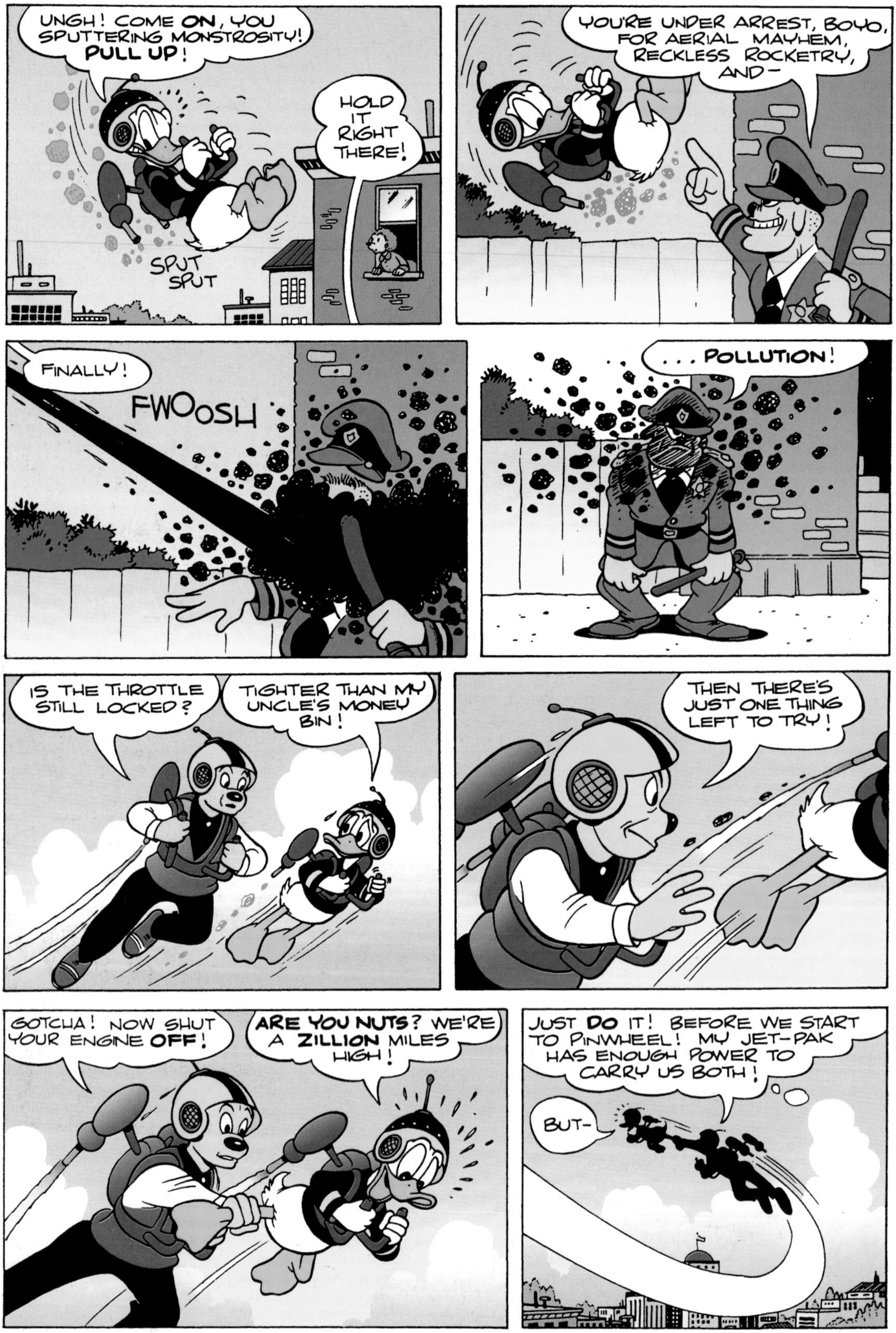
UNGH! COME ON, YOU SPUTTERING MONSTROSITY! PULL UP!
HOLD IT RIGHT THERE!
SPUT SPUT
YOU'RE UNDER ARREST, BOYO, FOR AERIAL MAYHEM, RECKLESS ROCKETRY, AND—
FINALLY!
FWOOSH
. . . POLLUTION!
IS THE THROTTLE STILL LOCKED?
TIGHTER THAN MY UNCLE'S MONEY BIN!
THEN THERE'S JUST ONE THING LEFT TO TRY!
GOTCHA! NOW SHUT YOUR ENGINE OFF!
ARE YOU NUTS? WE'RE A ZILLION MILES HIGH!
JUST DO IT! BEFORE WE START TO PINWHEEL! MY JET-PAK HAS ENOUGH POWER TO CARRY US BOTH!
BUT-

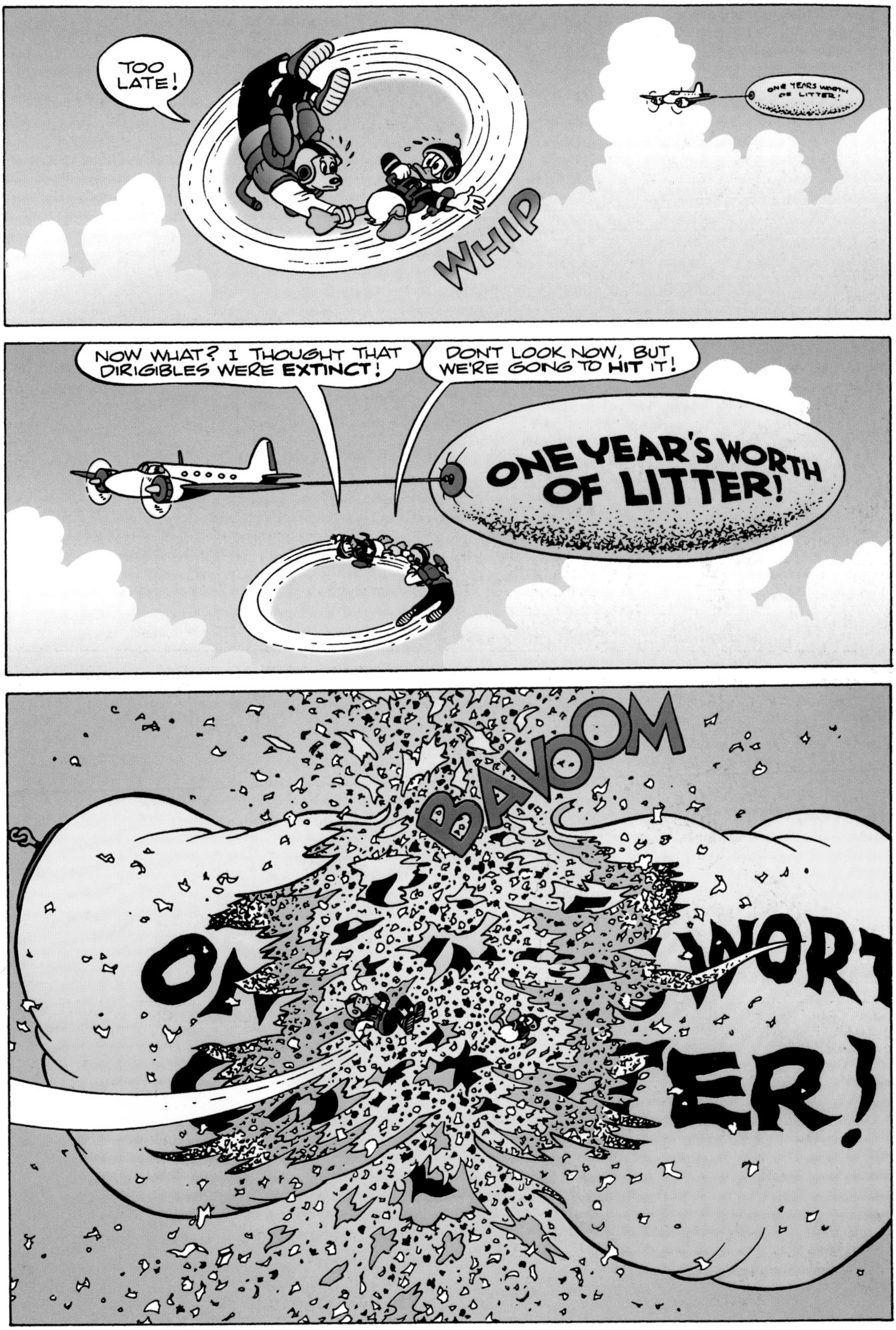
TOO LATE!
ONE YEARS WORTH OF LITTER!
WHIP
NOW WHAT? I THOUGHT THAT DIRIGIBLES WERE **EXTINCT**!
DON'T LOOK NOW, BUT WE'RE GOING TO **HIT** IT!
ONE YEAR'S WORTH OF LITTER!
BAVOOM

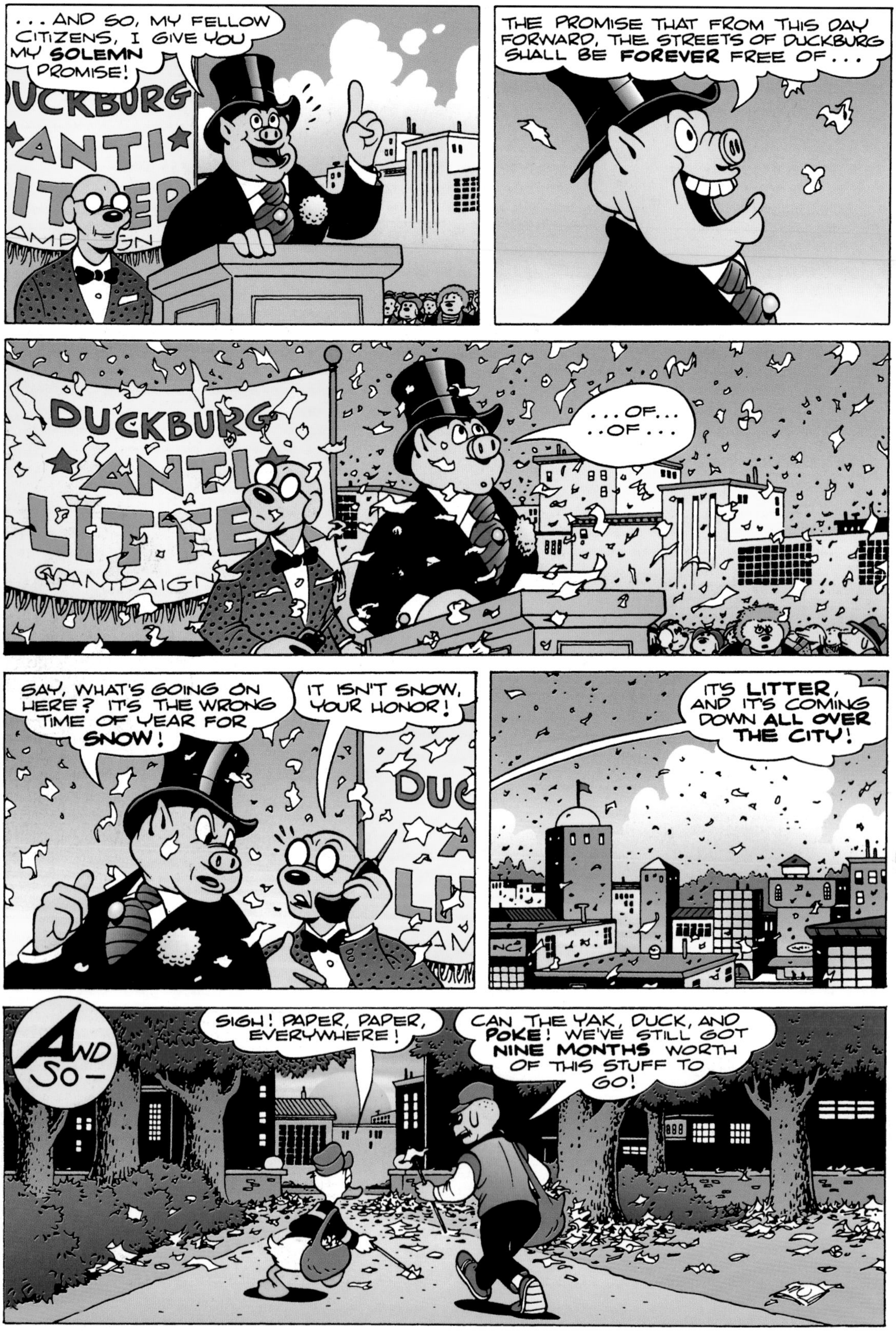
. . . AND SO, MY FELLOW CITIZENS, I GIVE YOU MY SOLEMN PROMISE!
DUCKBURG ANTI LITTER CAMPAIGN
THE PROMISE THAT FROM THIS DAY FORWARD, THE STREETS OF DUCKBURG SHALL BE FOREVER FREE OF . . .
DUCKBURG ANTI LITTE CAMPAIGN
. . . OF . . .
. . OF . . .
SAY, WHAT'S GOING ON HERE? IT'S THE WRONG TIME OF YEAR FOR SNOW!
IT ISN'T SNOW, YOUR HONOR!
IT'S LITTER, AND IT'S COMING DOWN ALL OVER THE CITY!
AND SO —
SIGH! PAPER, PAPER, EVERYWHERE!
CAN THE YAK, DUCK, AND POKE! WE'VE STILL GOT NINE MONTHS WORTH OF THIS STUFF TO GO!

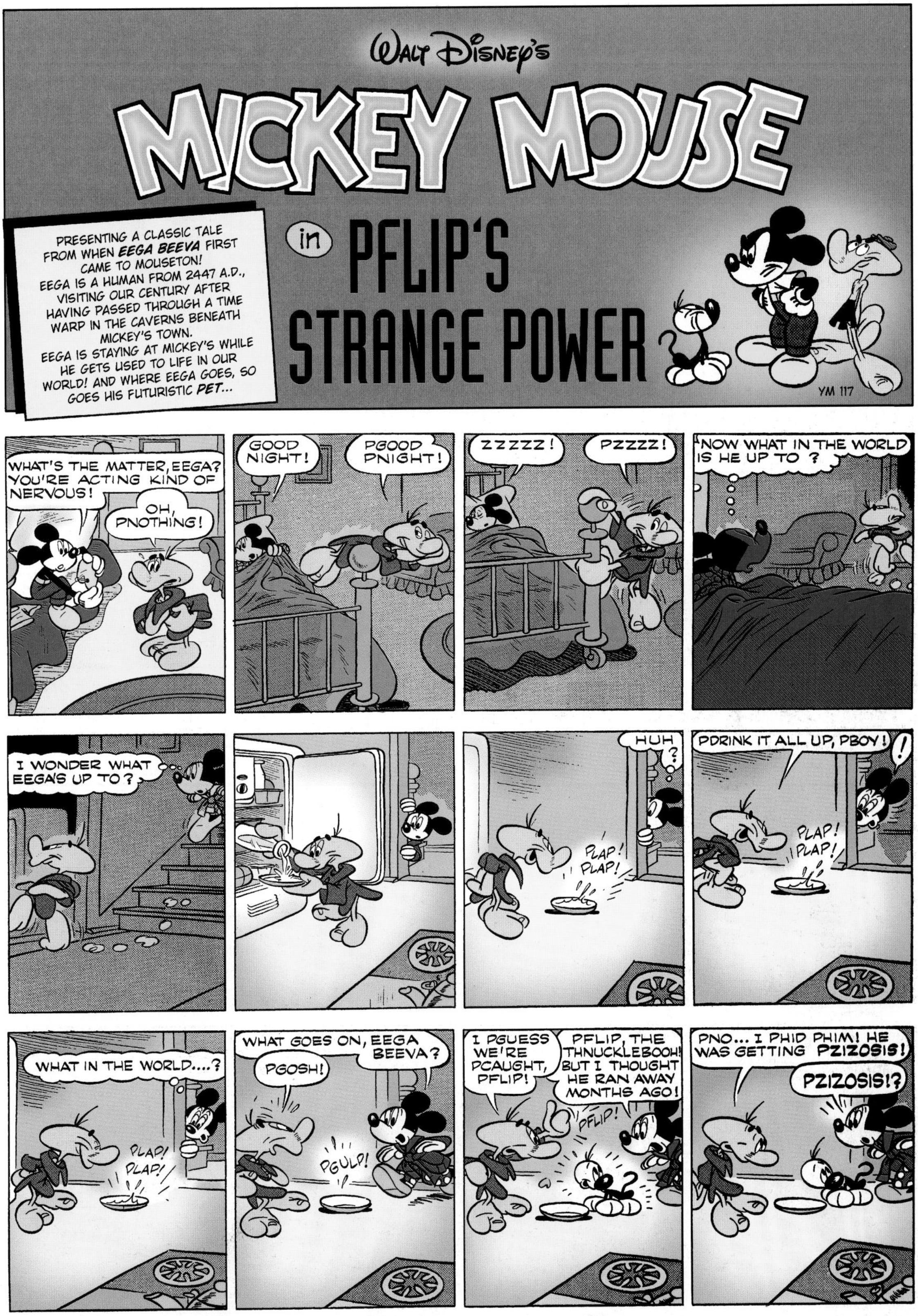
WALT DISNEY'S
MICKEY MOUSE
in PFLIP'S STRANGE POWER
PRESENTING A CLASSIC TALE FROM WHEN EEGA BEEVA FIRST CAME TO MOUSETON! EEGA IS A HUMAN FROM 2447 A.D., VISITING OUR CENTURY AFTER HAVING PASSED THROUGH A TIME WARP IN THE CAVERNS BENEATH MICKEY'S TOWN. EEGA IS STAYING AT MICKEY'S WHILE HE GETS USED TO LIFE IN OUR WORLD! AND WHERE EEGA GOES, SO GOES HIS FUTURISTIC PET...
YM 117
WHAT'S THE MATTER, EEGA? YOU'RE ACTING KIND OF NERVOUS!
OH, PNOTHING!
GOOD NIGHT!
PGOOD PNIGHT!
ZZZZZ!
PZZZZ!
NOW WHAT IN THE WORLD IS HE UP TO ?
I WONDER WHAT EEGA'S UP TO ?
HUH ?
PLAP! PLAP!
PDRINK IT ALL UP, PBOY!
!
PLAP! PLAP!
WHAT IN THE WORLD....?
PLAP! PLAP!
WHAT GOES ON, EEGA BEEVA?
PGOSH!
PGULP!
I PGUESS WE'RE PCAUGHT, PFLIP!
PFLIP, THE THNUCKLEBOOH! BUT I THOUGHT HE RAN AWAY MONTHS AGO!
PFLIP!
PNO... I PHID PHIM! HE WAS GETTING PZIZOSIS!
PZIZOSIS!?

MICKEY MOUSE

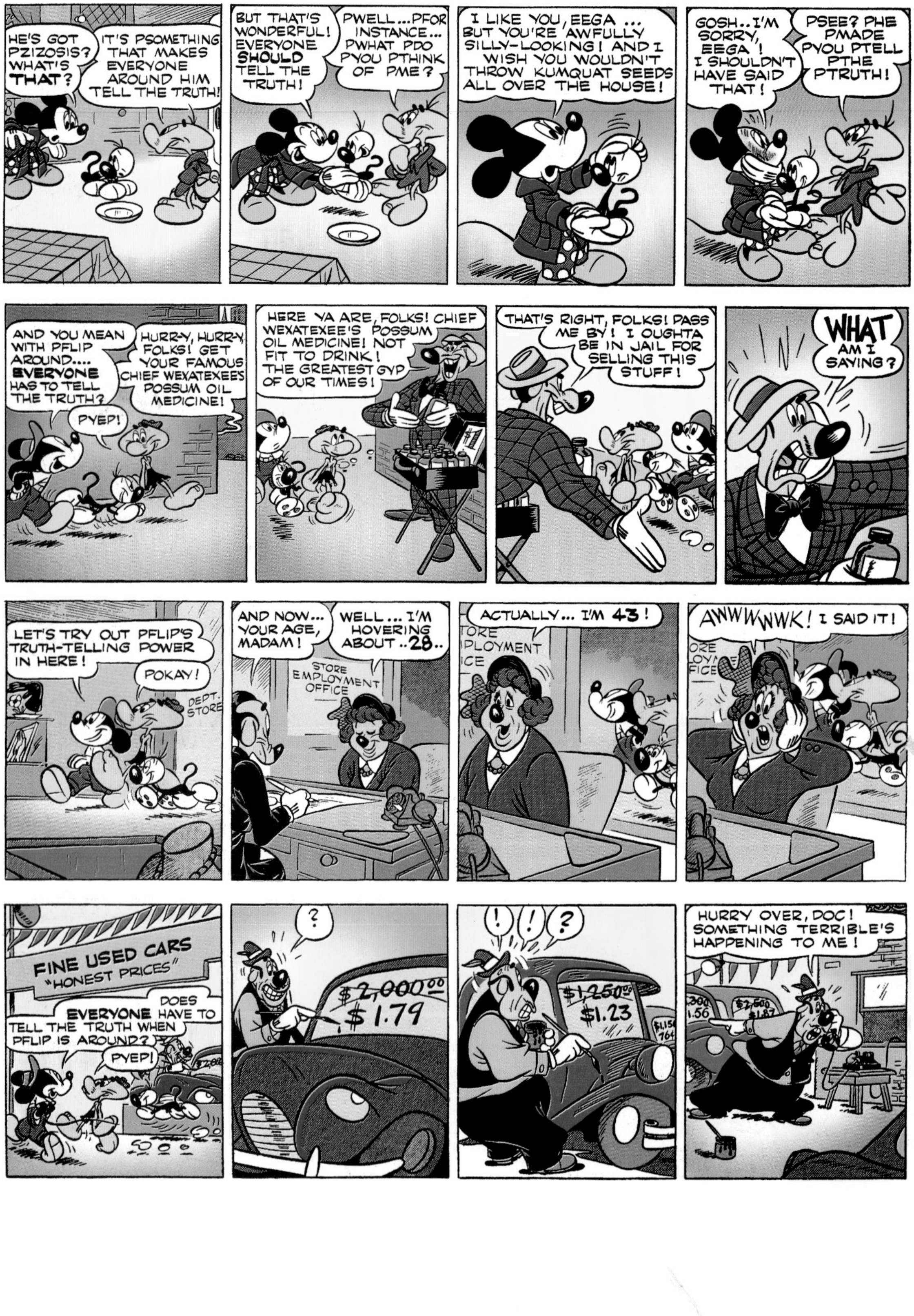
HE'S GOT PZIZOSIS? WHAT'S THAT?
IT'S PSOMETHING THAT MAKES EVERYONE AROUND HIM TELL THE TRUTH!
BUT THAT'S WONDERFUL! EVERYONE SHOULD TELL THE TRUTH!
PWELL...PFOR INSTANCE... PWHAT PDO PYOU PTHINK OF PME?
I LIKE YOU, EEGA ... BUT YOU'RE AWFULLY SILLY-LOOKING! AND I WISH YOU WOULDN'T THROW KUMQUAT SEEDS ALL OVER THE HOUSE!
GOSH..I'M SORRY, EEGA! I SHOULDN'T HAVE SAID THAT!
PSEE? PHE PMADE PYOU PTELL PTHE PTRUTH!
AND YOU MEAN WITH PFLIP AROUND.... EVERYONE HAS TO TELL THE TRUTH?
HURR-Y, HURR-Y, FOLKS! GET YOUR FAMOUS CHIEF WEXATEXEE'S POSSUM OIL MEDICINE!
PYEP!
HERE YA ARE, FOLKS! CHIEF WEXATEXEE'S POSSUM OIL MEDICINE! NOT FIT TO DRINK! THE GREATEST GYP OF OUR TIMES!
THAT'S RIGHT, FOLKS! PASS ME BY! I OUGHTA BE IN JAIL FOR SELLING THIS STUFF!
WHAT AM I SAYING?
LET'S TRY OUT PFLIP'S TRUTH-TELLING POWER IN HERE!
POKAY!
DEPT. STORE
AND NOW... YOUR AGE, MADAM!
WELL... I'M HOVERING ABOUT ..28..
STORE EMPLOYMENT OFFICE
ACTUALLY... I'M 43!
AWWWWWK! I SAID IT!
FINE USED CARS "HONEST PRICES"
DOES EVERYONE HAVE TO TELL THE TRUTH WHEN PFLIP IS AROUND?
PYEP!
?
$2,000.00
$1.79
! ! ?
$1,250.00
$1.23
HURRY OVER, DOC! SOMETHING TERRIBLE'S HAPPENING TO ME!

PFLIP'S STRANGE POWER

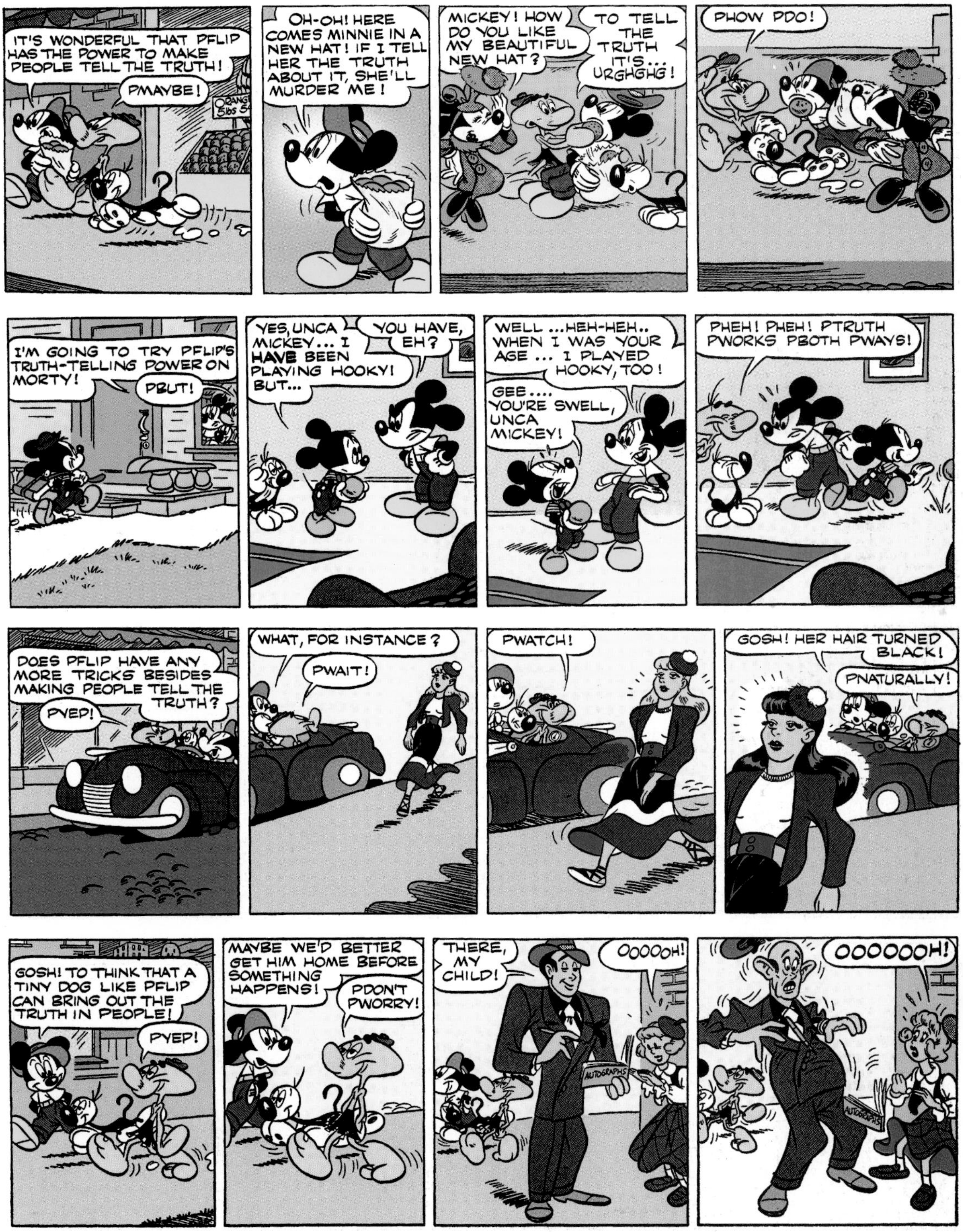
IT'S WONDERFUL THAT PFLIP HAS THE POWER TO MAKE PEOPLE TELL THE TRUTH!
PMAYBE!
OH-OH! HERE COMES MINNIE IN A NEW HAT! IF I TELL HER THE TRUTH ABOUT IT, SHE'LL MURDER ME!
MICKEY! HOW DO YOU LIKE MY BEAUTIFUL NEW HAT?
TO TELL THE TRUTH IT'S... URGHGHG!
PHOW PDO!
I'M GOING TO TRY PFLIP'S TRUTH-TELLING POWER ON MORTY!
PBUT!
YES, UNCA MICKEY... I HAVE BEEN PLAYING HOOKY! BUT...
YOU HAVE, EH?
WELL ...HEH-HEH.. WHEN I WAS YOUR AGE ... I PLAYED HOOKY, TOO!
GEE.... YOU'RE SWELL, UNCA MICKEY!
PHEH! PHEH! PTRUTH PWORKS PBOTH PWAYS!
DOES PFLIP HAVE ANY MORE TRICKS BESIDES MAKING PEOPLE TELL THE TRUTH?
PYEP!
WHAT, FOR INSTANCE?
PWAIT!
PWATCH!
GOSH! HER HAIR TURNED BLACK!
PNATURALLY!
GOSH! TO THINK THAT A TINY DOG LIKE PFLIP CAN BRING OUT THE TRUTH IN PEOPLE!
PYEP!
MAYBE WE'D BETTER GET HIM HOME BEFORE SOMETHING HAPPENS!
PDON'T PWORRY!
THERE, MY CHILD!
OOOOOH!
AUTOGRAPHS
OOOOOOH!
AUTOGRAPHS

MICKEY MOUSE

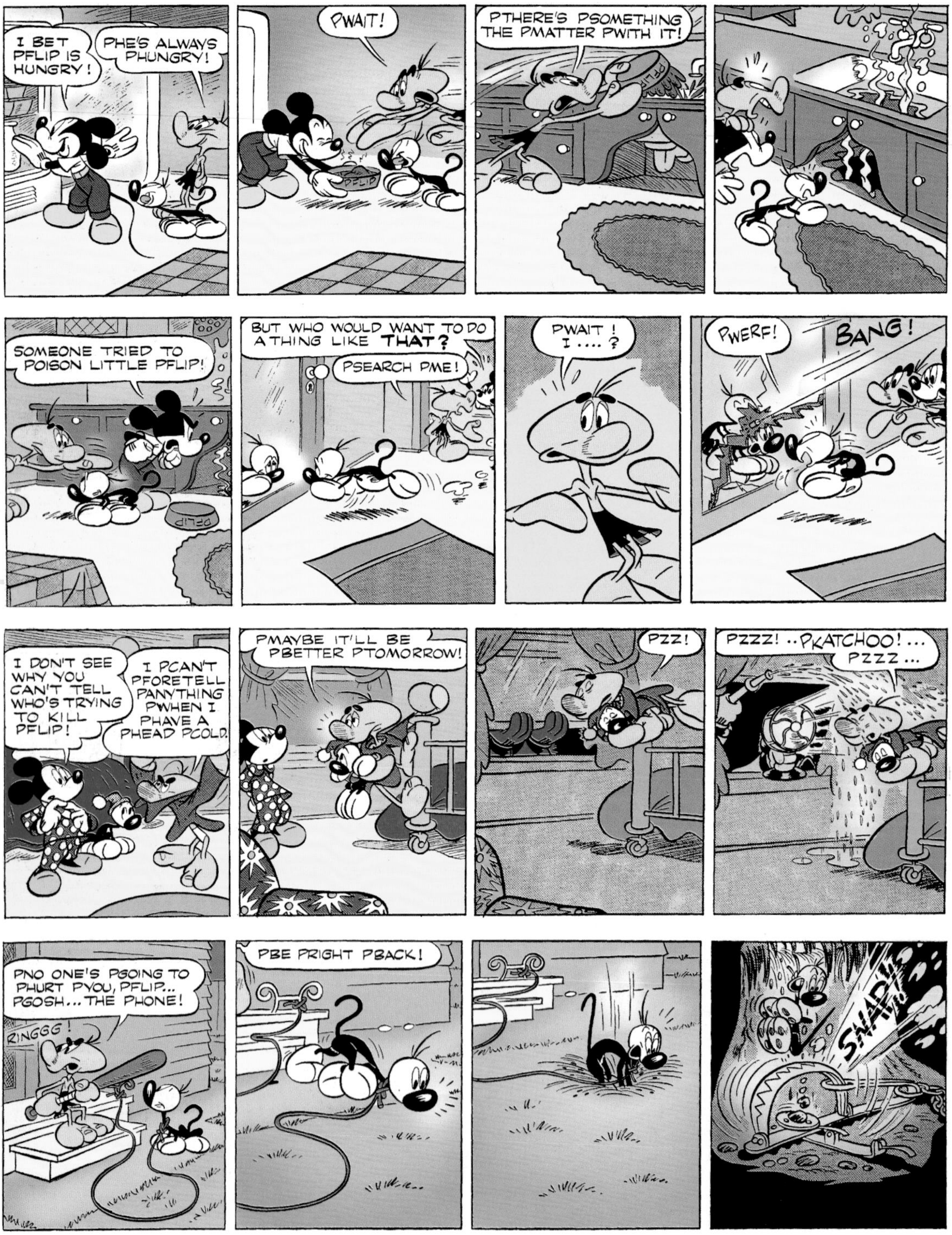
I BET PFLIP IS HUNGRY!
PHE'S ALWAYS PHUNGRY!
PWAIT!
PTHERE'S PSOMETHING THE PMATTER PWITH IT!
SOMEONE TRIED TO POISON LITTLE PFLIP!
BUT WHO WOULD WANT TO DO A THING LIKE THAT?
PSEARCH PME!
PWAIT! I....?
PWERF!
BANG!
I DON'T SEE WHY YOU CAN'T TELL WHO'S TRYING TO KILL PFLIP!
I PCAN'T PFORETELL PANYTHING PWHEN I PHAVE A PHEAD PCOLD.
PMAYBE IT'LL BE PBETTER PTOMORROW!
PZZ!
PZZZ! ..PKATCHOO!... PZZZ...
PNO ONE'S PGOING TO PHURT PYOU, PFLIP... PGOSH... THE PHONE!
RINGGG!
PBE PRIGHT PBACK!
SNAP!!

PFLIP'S STRANGE POWER

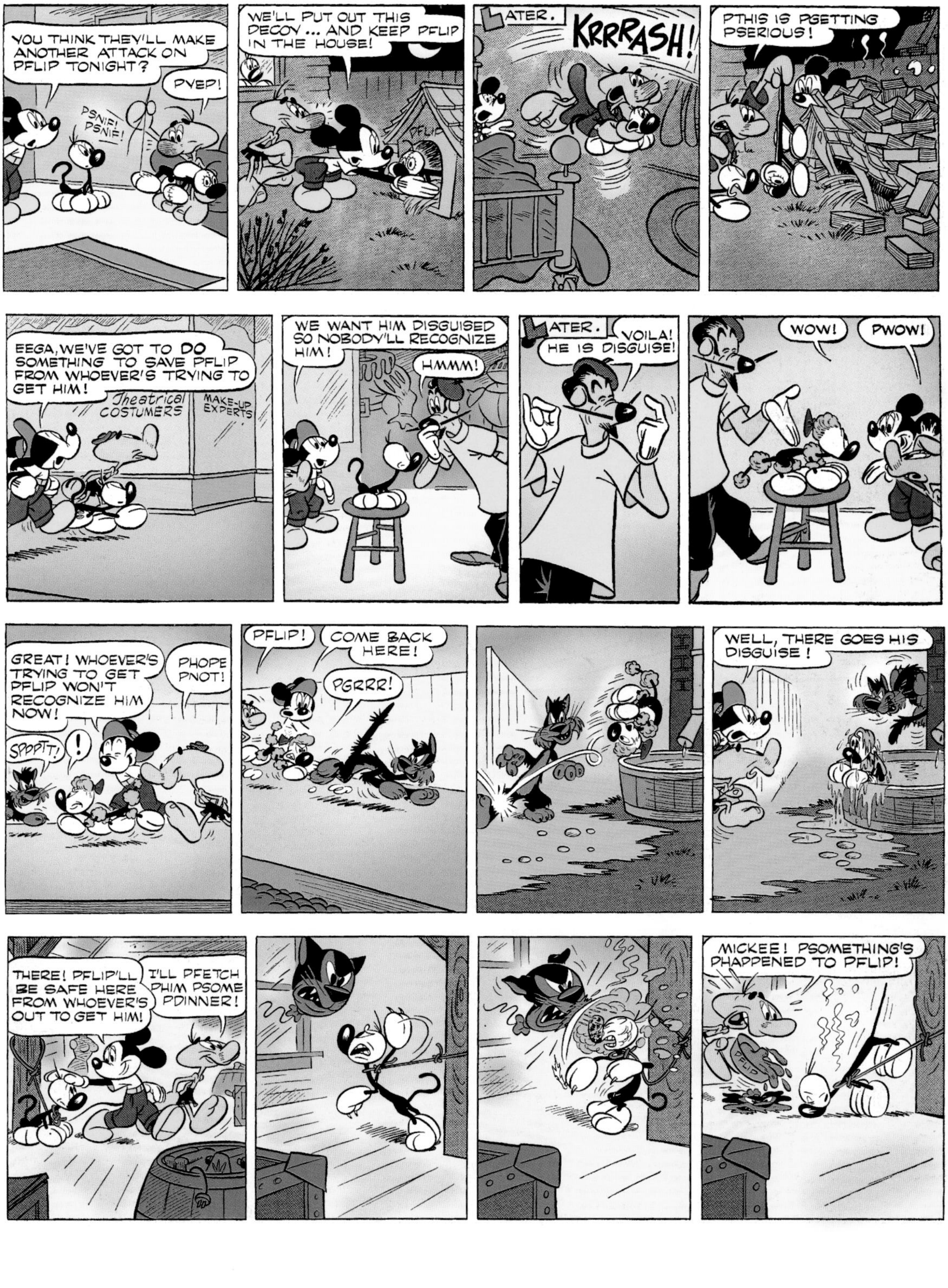
YOU THINK THEY'LL MAKE ANOTHER ATTACK ON PFLIP TONIGHT?
PSNIF! PSNIF!
PYEP!
WE'LL PUT OUT THIS DECOY ... AND KEEP PFLIP IN THE HOUSE!
PFLIP
LATER.
KRRRASH!
PTHIS IS PGETTING PSERIOUS!
EEGA, WE'VE GOT TO DO SOMETHING TO SAVE PFLIP FROM WHOEVER'S TRYING TO GET HIM!
Theatrical COSTUMERS
MAKE-UP EXPERTS
WE WANT HIM DISGUISED SO NOBODY'LL RECOGNIZE HIM!
HMMM!
LATER.
VOILA! HE IS DISGUISE!
WOW!
PWOW!
GREAT! WHOEVER'S TRYING TO GET PFLIP WON'T RECOGNIZE HIM NOW!
PHOPE PNOT!
SPPPTT!
!
PFLIP!
COME BACK HERE!
PGRRR!
WELL, THERE GOES HIS DISGUISE!
THERE! PFLIP'LL BE SAFE HERE FROM WHOEVER'S OUT TO GET HIM!
I'LL PFETCH PHIM PSOME PDINNER!
MICKEE! PSOMETHING'S PHAPPENED TO PFLIP!
PFLIP

MICKEY MOUSE

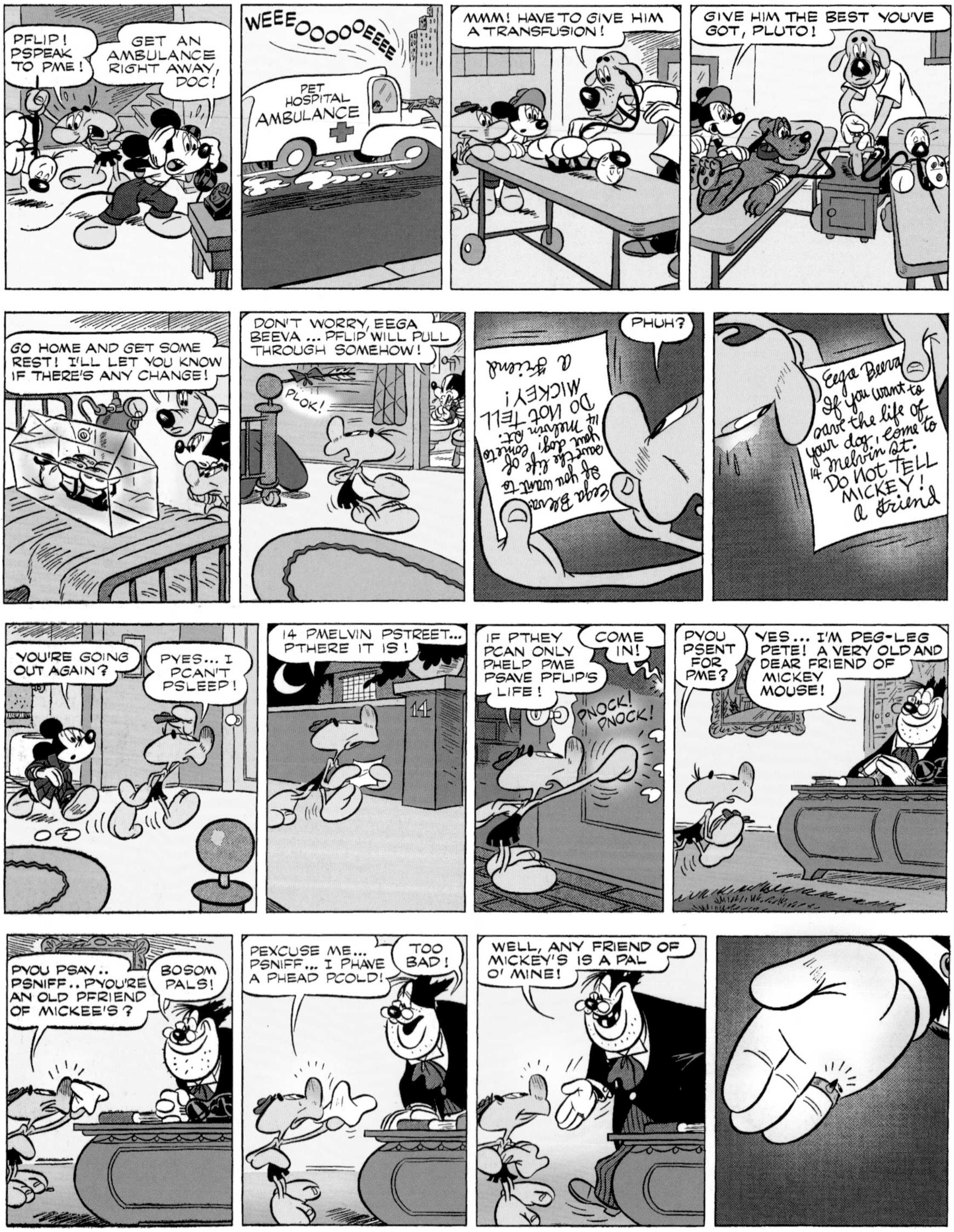
PFLIP! PSPEAK TO PME!
GET AN AMBULANCE RIGHT AWAY, DOC!
WEEEOOOOOEEEE
PET HOSPITAL AMBULANCE
MMM! HAVE TO GIVE HIM A TRANSFUSION!
GIVE HIM THE BEST YOU'VE GOT, PLUTO!
GO HOME AND GET SOME REST! I'LL LET YOU KNOW IF THERE'S ANY CHANGE!
DON'T WORRY, EEGA BEEVA ... PFLIP WILL PULL THROUGH SOMEHOW!
PLOK!
PHUH?
Eega Beeva If you want to save the life of your dog, come to 14 Melvin St. DO NOT TELL MICKEY! A Friend
YOU'RE GOING OUT AGAIN?
PYES... I PCAN'T PSLEEP!
14 PMELVIN PSTREET... PTHERE IT IS!
14
IF PTHEY PCAN ONLY PHELP PME PSAVE PFLIP'S LIFE!
COME IN!
PNOCK! PNOCK!
PYOU PSENT FOR PME?
YES... I'M PEG-LEG PETE! A VERY OLD AND DEAR FRIEND OF MICKEY MOUSE!
PYOU PSAY.. PSNIFF.. PYOU'RE AN OLD PFRIEND OF MICKEE'S?
BOSOM PALS!
PEXCUSE ME... PSNIFF... I PHAVE A PHEAD PCOLD!
TOO BAD!
WELL, ANY FRIEND OF MICKEY'S IS A PAL O' MINE!

PFLIP'S STRANGE POWER

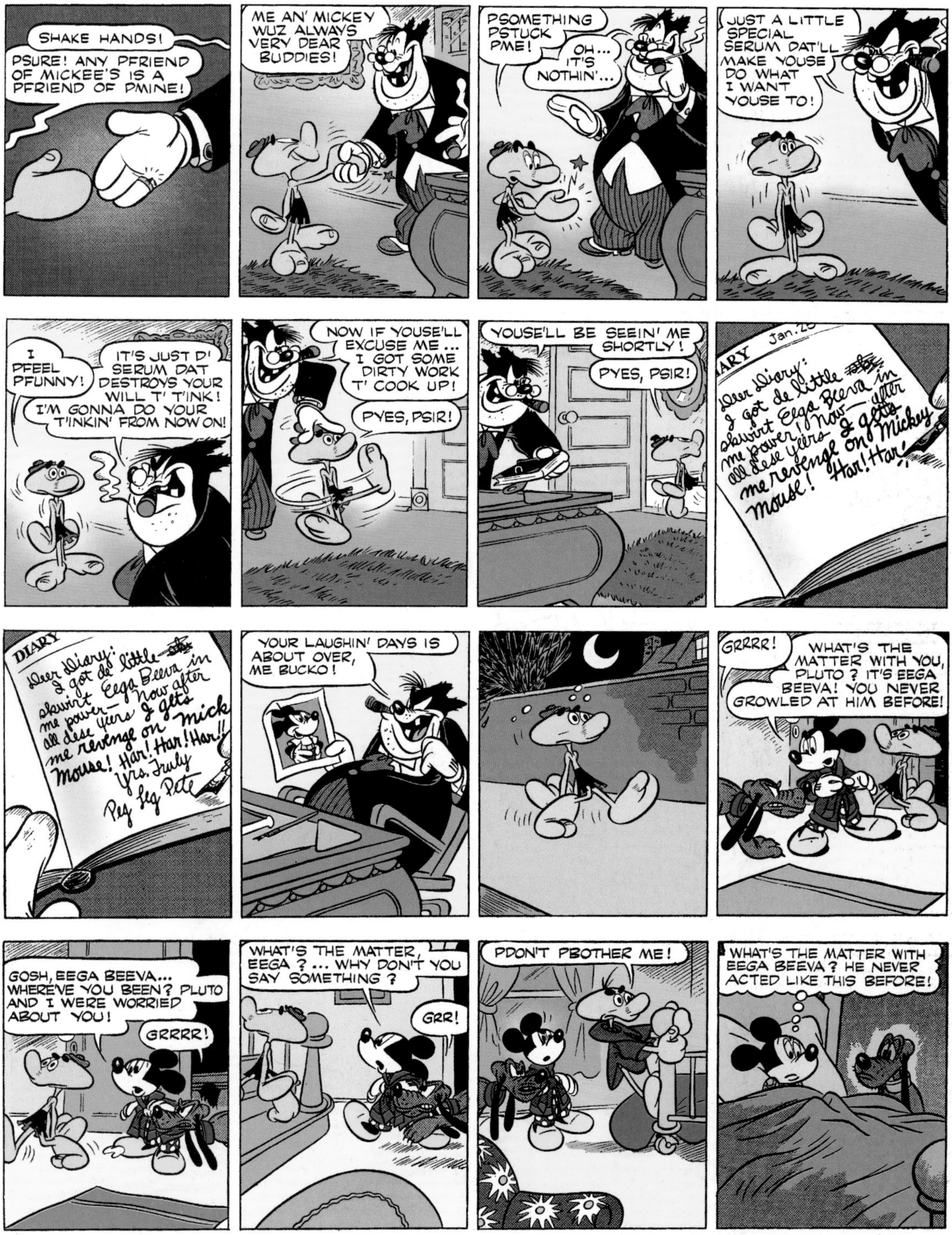
SHAKE HANDS!
PSURE! ANY PFRIEND OF MICKEE'S IS A PFRIEND OF PMINE!
ME AN' MICKEY WUZ ALWAYS VERY DEAR BUDDIES!
PSOMETHING PSTUCK PME!
OH... IT'S NOTHIN'...
JUST A LITTLE SPECIAL SERUM DAT'LL MAKE YOUSE DO WHAT I WANT YOUSE TO!
I PFEEL PFUNNY!
IT'S JUST D' SERUM DAT DESTROYS YOUR WILL T' T'INK!
I'M GONNA DO YOUR T'INKIN' FROM NOW ON!
NOW IF YOUSE'LL EXCUSE ME ... I GOT SOME DIRTY WORK T' COOK UP!
PYES, PSIR!
YOUSE'LL BE SEEIN' ME SHORTLY!
PYES, PSIR!
DIARY
Deer Diary: I got de little skwirt Eega Beeva in me power! Now after all dese yeers I gets me revenge on Mickey Mouse! Har! Har!
DIARY
Deer Diary: I got de little skwirt Eega Beeva in me power — Now after all dese yeers I gets me revenge on mick Mouse! Har! Har! Har!!
Yrs. Truly
Peg Leg Pete
YOUR LAUGHIN' DAYS IS ABOUT OVER, ME BUCKO!
GRRRR!
WHAT'S THE MATTER WITH YOU, PLUTO? IT'S EEGA BEEVA! YOU NEVER GROWLED AT HIM BEFORE!
GOSH, EEGA BEEVA... WHERE'VE YOU BEEN? PLUTO AND I WERE WORRIED ABOUT YOU!
GRRRR!
WHAT'S THE MATTER, EEGA? ... WHY DON'T YOU SAY SOMETHING?
GRR!
PDON'T PBOTHER ME!
WHAT'S THE MATTER WITH EEGA BEEVA? HE NEVER ACTED LIKE THIS BEFORE!

MICKEY MOUSE

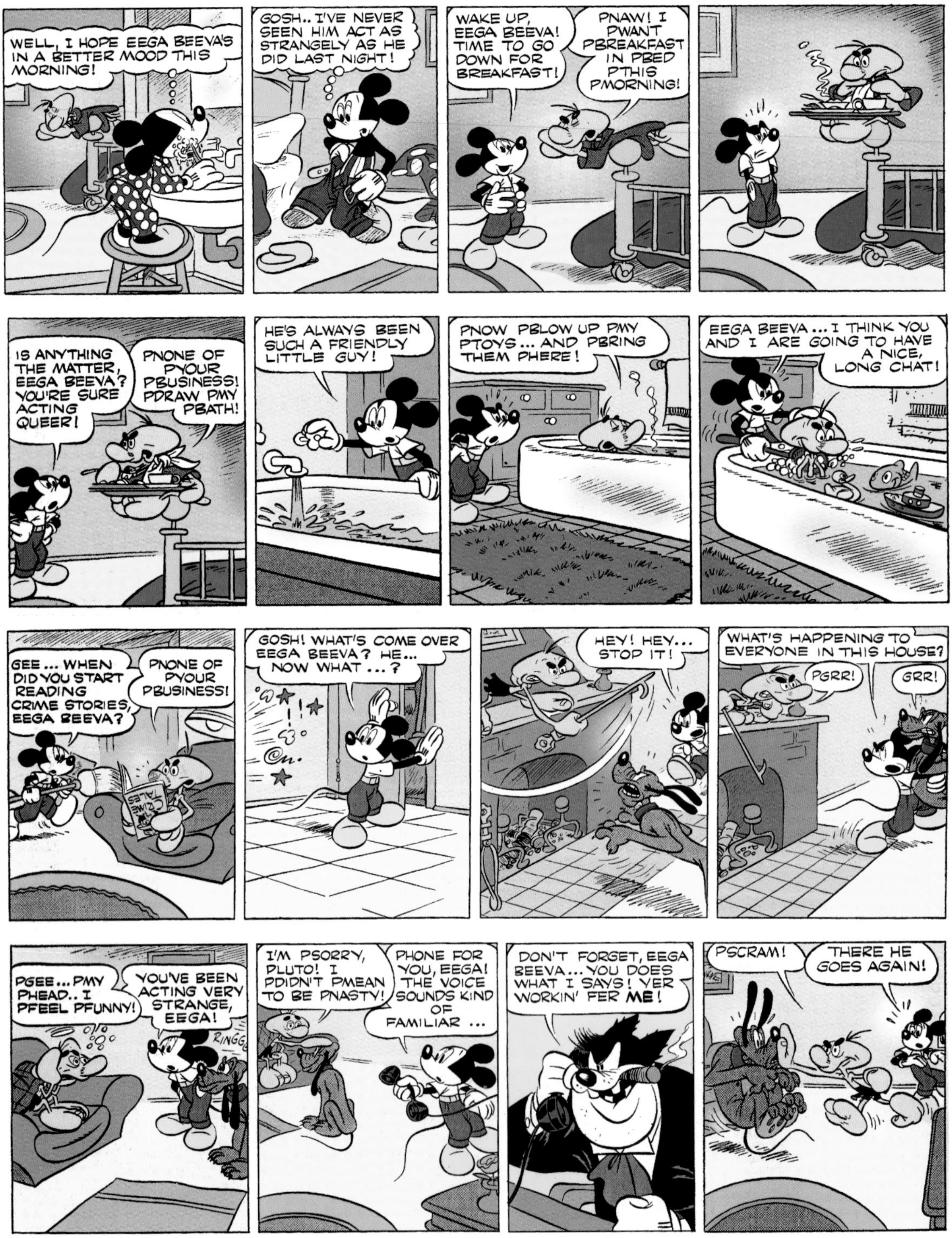
WELL, I HOPE EEGA BEEVA'S IN A BETTER MOOD THIS MORNING!
GOSH.. I'VE NEVER SEEN HIM ACT AS STRANGELY AS HE DID LAST NIGHT!
WAKE UP, EEGA BEEVA! TIME TO GO DOWN FOR BREAKFAST!
PNAW! I PWANT PBREAKFAST IN PBED PTHIS PMORNING!
IS ANYTHING THE MATTER, EEGA BEEVA? YOU'RE SURE ACTING QUEER!
PNONE OF PYOUR PBUSINESS! PDRAW PMY PBATH!
HE'S ALWAYS BEEN SUCH A FRIENDLY LITTLE GUY!
PNOW PBLOW UP PMY PTOYS... AND PBRING THEM PHERE!
EEGA BEEVA... I THINK YOU AND I ARE GOING TO HAVE A NICE, LONG CHAT!
GEE... WHEN DID YOU START READING CRIME STORIES, EEGA BEEVA?
PNONE OF PYOUR PBUSINESS!
CRIME TALES
GOSH! WHAT'S COME OVER EEGA BEEVA? HE... NOW WHAT...?
HEY! HEY... STOP IT!
WHAT'S HAPPENING TO EVERYONE IN THIS HOUSE?
PGRR!
GRR!
PGEE... PMY PHEAD.. I PFEEL PFUNNY!
YOU'VE BEEN ACTING VERY STRANGE, EEGA!
RINGG
I'M PSORRY, PLUTO! I PDIDN'T PMEAN TO BE PNASTY!
PHONE FOR YOU, EEGA! THE VOICE SOUNDS KIND OF FAMILIAR...
DON'T FORGET, EEGA BEEVA... YOU DOES WHAT I SAYS! YER WORKIN' FER ME!
PSCRAM!
THERE HE GOES AGAIN!

PFLIP'S STRANGE POWER

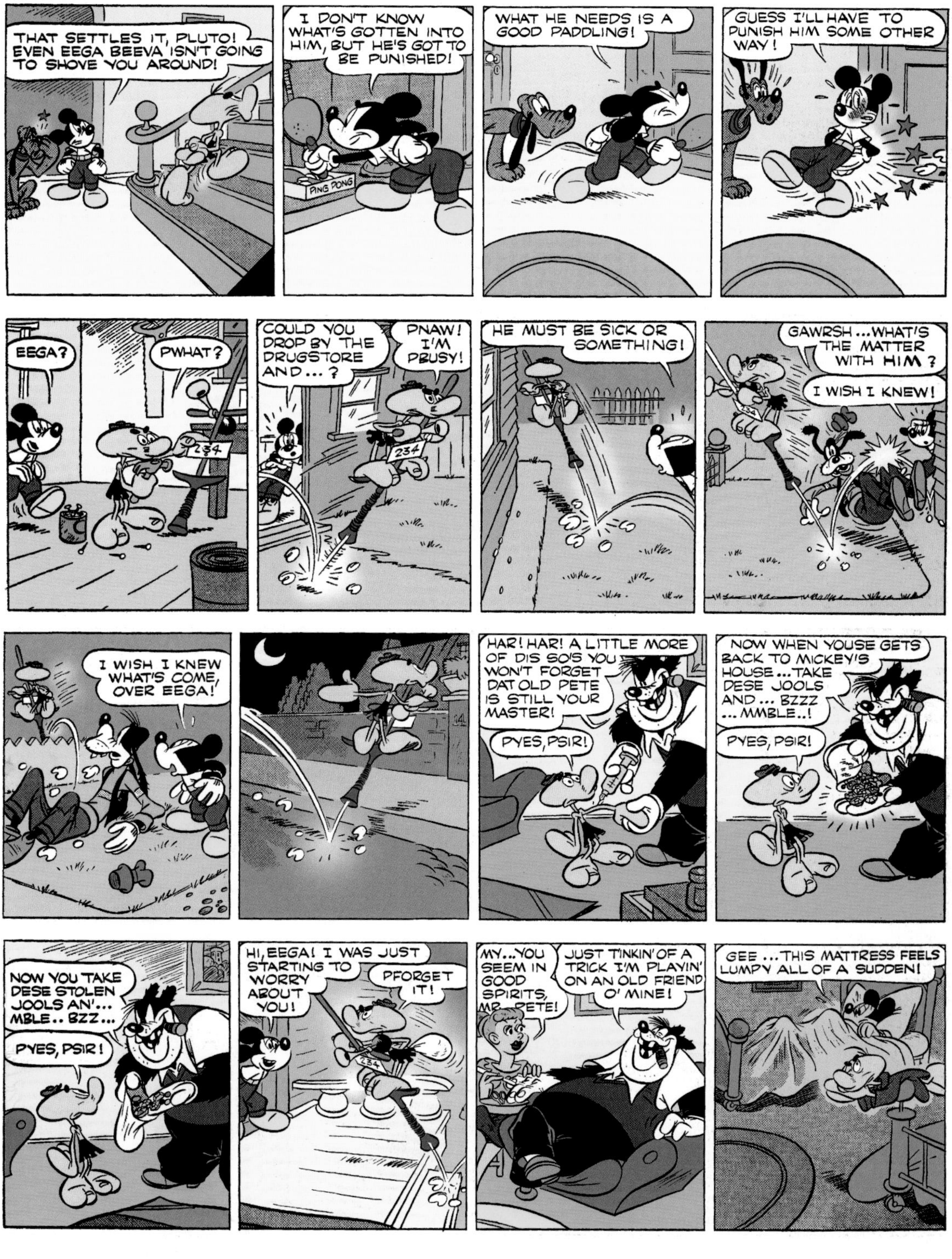

THAT SETTLES IT, PLUTO! EVEN EEGA BEEVA ISN'T GOING TO SHOVE YOU AROUND!
I DON'T KNOW WHAT'S GOTTEN INTO HIM, BUT HE'S GOT TO BE PUNISHED!
PING PONG
WHAT HE NEEDS IS A GOOD PADDLING!
GUESS I'LL HAVE TO PUNISH HIM SOME OTHER WAY!
EEGA?
PWHAT?
234
COULD YOU DROP BY THE DRUGSTORE AND...?
PNAW! I'M PBUSY!
234
HE MUST BE SICK OR SOMETHING!
GAWRSH...WHAT'S THE MATTER WITH HIM?
I WISH I KNEW!
I WISH I KNEW WHAT'S COME OVER EEGA!
HAR! HAR! A LITTLE MORE OF DIS SO'S YOU WON'T FORGET DAT OLD PETE IS STILL YOUR MASTER!
PYES, PSIR!
NOW WHEN YOUSE GETS BACK TO MICKEY'S HOUSE...TAKE DESE JOOLS AND... BZZZ ...MMBLE..!
PYES, PSIR!
NOW YOU TAKE DESE STOLEN JOOLS AN'... MBLE.. BZZ...
PYES, PSIR!
HI, EEGA! I WAS JUST STARTING TO WORRY ABOUT YOU!
PFORGET IT!
MY...YOU SEEM IN GOOD SPIRITS, MR. PETE!
JUST TINKIN' OF A TRICK I'M PLAYIN' ON AN OLD FRIEND O' MINE!
GEE...THIS MATTRESS FEELS LUMPY ALL OF A SUDDEN!

MICKEY MOUSE

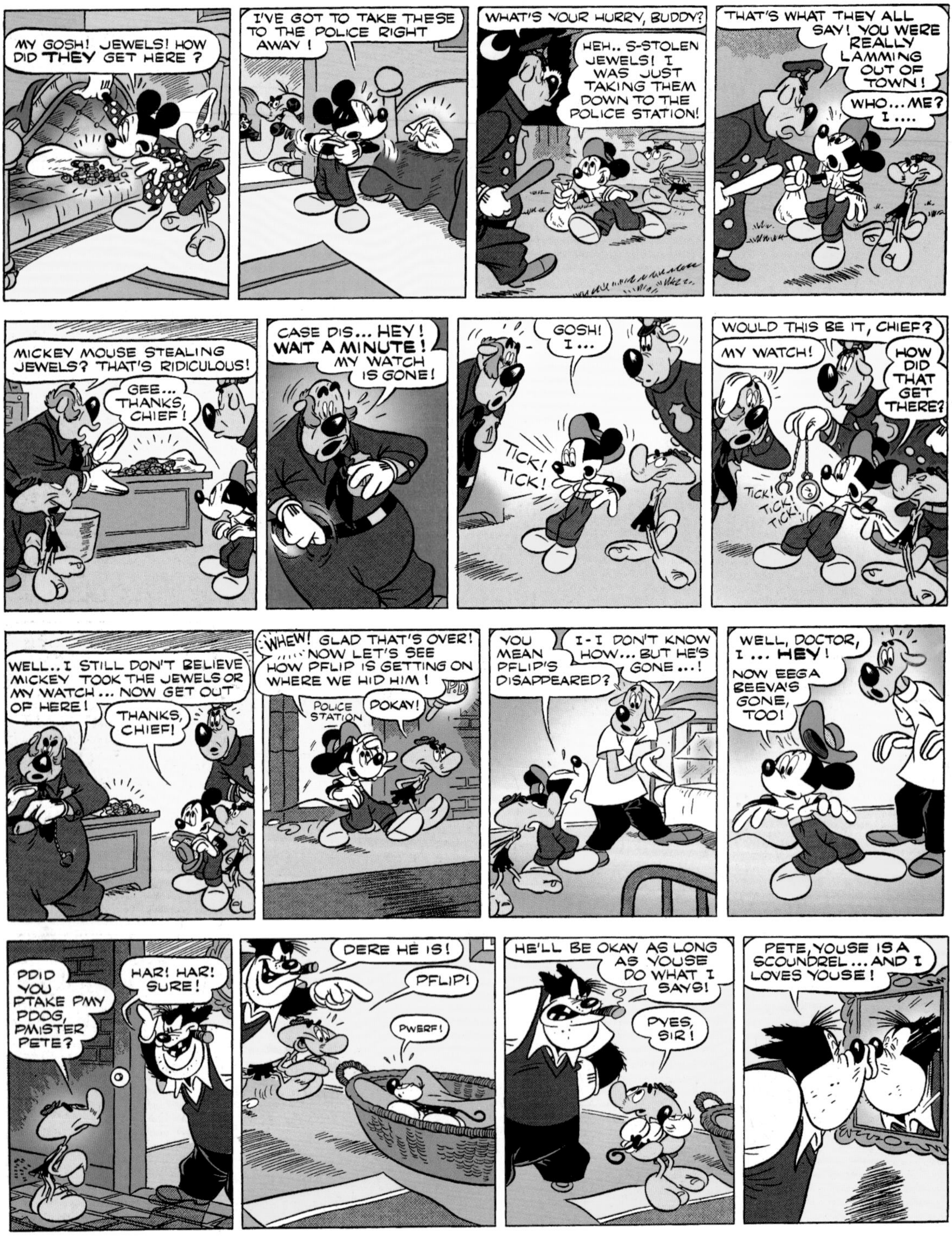
MY GOSH! JEWELS! HOW DID THEY GET HERE ?
I'VE GOT TO TAKE THESE TO THE POLICE RIGHT AWAY !
WHAT'S YOUR HURRY, BUDDY?
HEH.. S-STOLEN JEWELS! I WAS JUST TAKING THEM DOWN TO THE POLICE STATION!
THAT'S WHAT THEY ALL SAY! YOU WERE REALLY LAMMING OUT OF TOWN!
WHO... ME? I ....
MICKEY MOUSE STEALING JEWELS? THAT'S RIDICULOUS!
GEE... THANKS, CHIEF!
CASE DIS... HEY! WAIT A MINUTE! MY WATCH IS GONE!
GOSH! I ...
TICK! TICK!
WOULD THIS BE IT, CHIEF?
MY WATCH!
HOW DID THAT GET THERE?
TICK! TICK! TICK!
WELL.. I STILL DON'T BELIEVE MICKEY TOOK THE JEWELS OR MY WATCH ... NOW GET OUT OF HERE!
THANKS, CHIEF!
WHEW! GLAD THAT'S OVER! NOW LET'S SEE HOW PFLIP IS GETTING ON WHERE WE HID HIM !
POLICE STATION
POKAY!
YOU MEAN PFLIP'S DISAPPEARED?
I-I DON'T KNOW HOW... BUT HE'S GONE...!
WELL, DOCTOR, I ... HEY!
NOW EEGA BEEVA'S GONE, TOO!
PDID YOU PTAKE PMY PDOG, PMISTER PETE?
HAR! HAR! SURE!
DERE HE IS!
PFLIP!
PWERF!
HE'LL BE OKAY AS LONG AS YOUSE DO WHAT I SAYS!
PYES, SIR!
PETE, YOUSE IS A SCOUNDREL... AND I LOVES YOUSE!

PFLIP'S STRANGE POWER

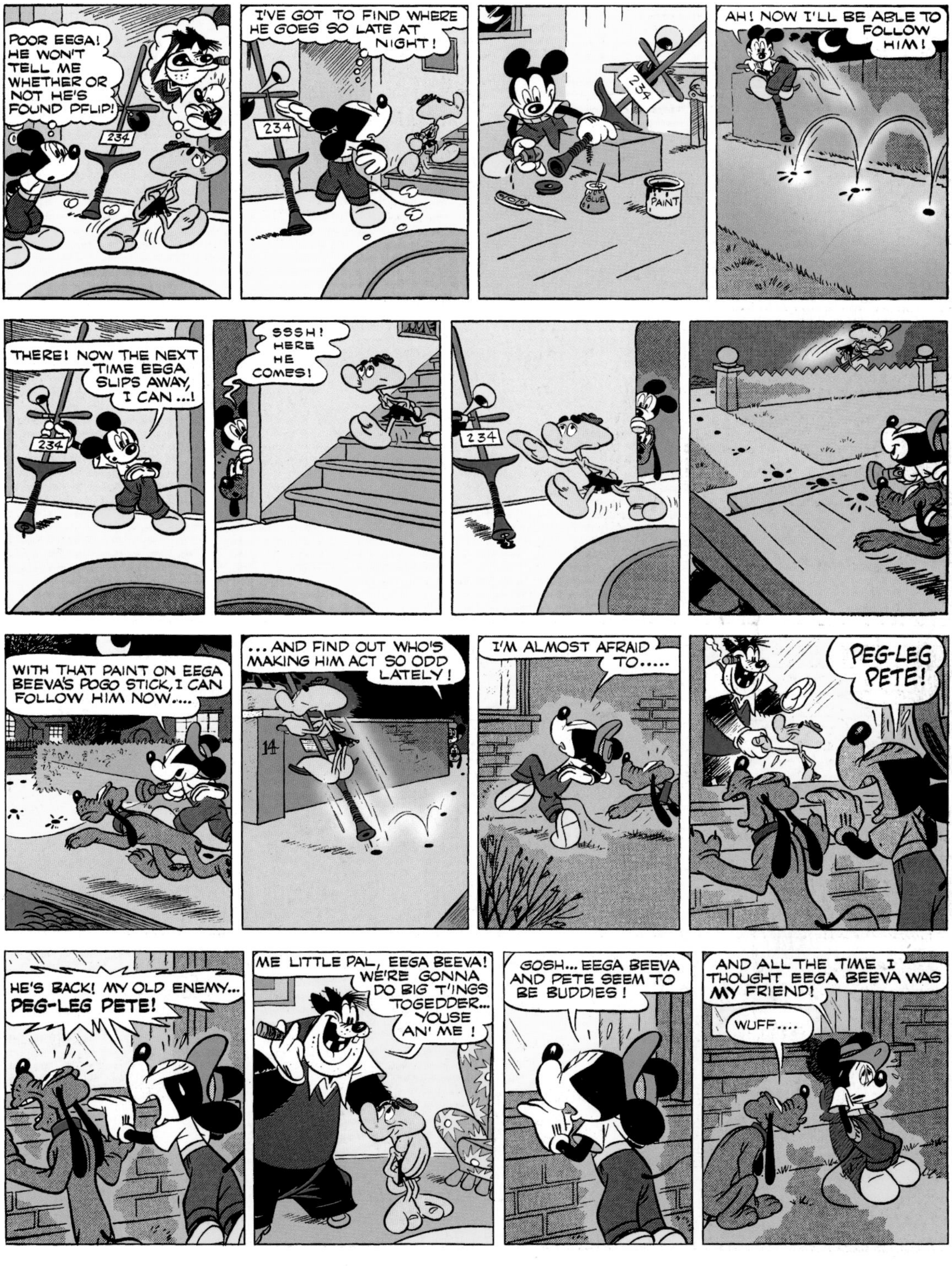

POOR EEGA! HE WON'T TELL ME WHETHER OR NOT HE'S FOUND PFLIP!
234
I'VE GOT TO FIND WHERE HE GOES SO LATE AT NIGHT!
234
234
GLUE
PAINT
AH! NOW I'LL BE ABLE TO FOLLOW HIM!
THERE! NOW THE NEXT TIME EEGA SLIPS AWAY, I CAN ...!
234
SSSH! HERE HE COMES!
234
WITH THAT PAINT ON EEGA BEEVA'S POGO STICK, I CAN FOLLOW HIM NOW....
...AND FIND OUT WHO'S MAKING HIM ACT SO ODD LATELY!
14
I'M ALMOST AFRAID TO.....
PEG-LEG PETE!
HE'S BACK! MY OLD ENEMY... PEG-LEG PETE!
ME LITTLE PAL, EEGA BEEVA! WE'RE GONNA DO BIG T'INGS TOGEDDER... YOUSE AN' ME!
GOSH... EEGA BEEVA AND PETE SEEM TO BE BUDDIES!
AND ALL THE TIME I THOUGHT EEGA BEEVA WAS MY FRIEND!
WUFF....

MICKEY MOUSE

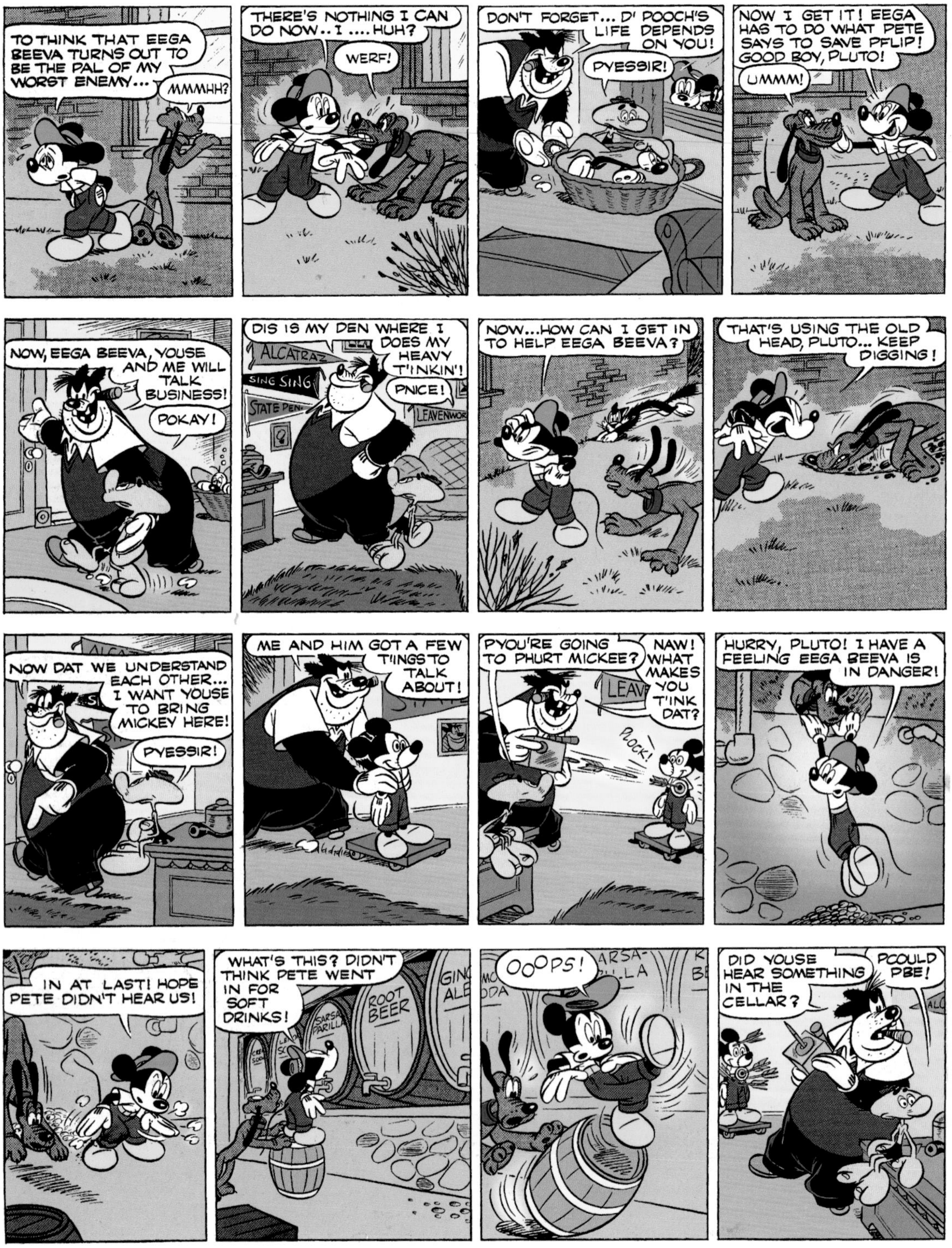

TO THINK THAT EEGA BEEVA TURNS OUT TO BE THE PAL OF MY WORST ENEMY...
MMMHH?
THERE'S NOTHING I CAN DO NOW.. I .... HUH?
WERF!
DON'T FORGET... D' POOCH'S LIFE DEPENDS ON YOU!
PYESSIR!
NOW I GET IT! EEGA HAS TO DO WHAT PETE SAYS TO SAVE PFLIP! GOOD BOY, PLUTO!
UMMM!
NOW, EEGA BEEVA, YOUSE AND ME WILL TALK BUSINESS!
POKAY!
DIS IS MY DEN WHERE I DOES MY HEAVY T'INKIN'!
ALCATRAZ
SING SING
STATE PEN
LEAVENWOR
PNICE!
NOW...HOW CAN I GET IN TO HELP EEGA BEEVA?
THAT'S USING THE OLD HEAD, PLUTO... KEEP DIGGING!
NOW DAT WE UNDERSTAND EACH OTHER... I WANT YOUSE TO BRING MICKEY HERE!
PYESSIR!
ME AND HIM GOT A FEW T'INGS TO TALK ABOUT!
PYOU'RE GOING TO PHURT MICKEE?
NAW! WHAT MAKES YOU T'INK DAT?
PLOCK!
HURRY, PLUTO! I HAVE A FEELING EEGA BEEVA IS IN DANGER!
IN AT LAST! HOPE PETE DIDN'T HEAR US!
WHAT'S THIS? DIDN'T THINK PETE WENT IN FOR SOFT DRINKS!
SARSA-PARILLA
ROOT BEER
OOOPS!
DID YOUSE HEAR SOMETHING IN THE CELLAR?
PCOULD PBE!

PFLIP'S STRANGE POWER

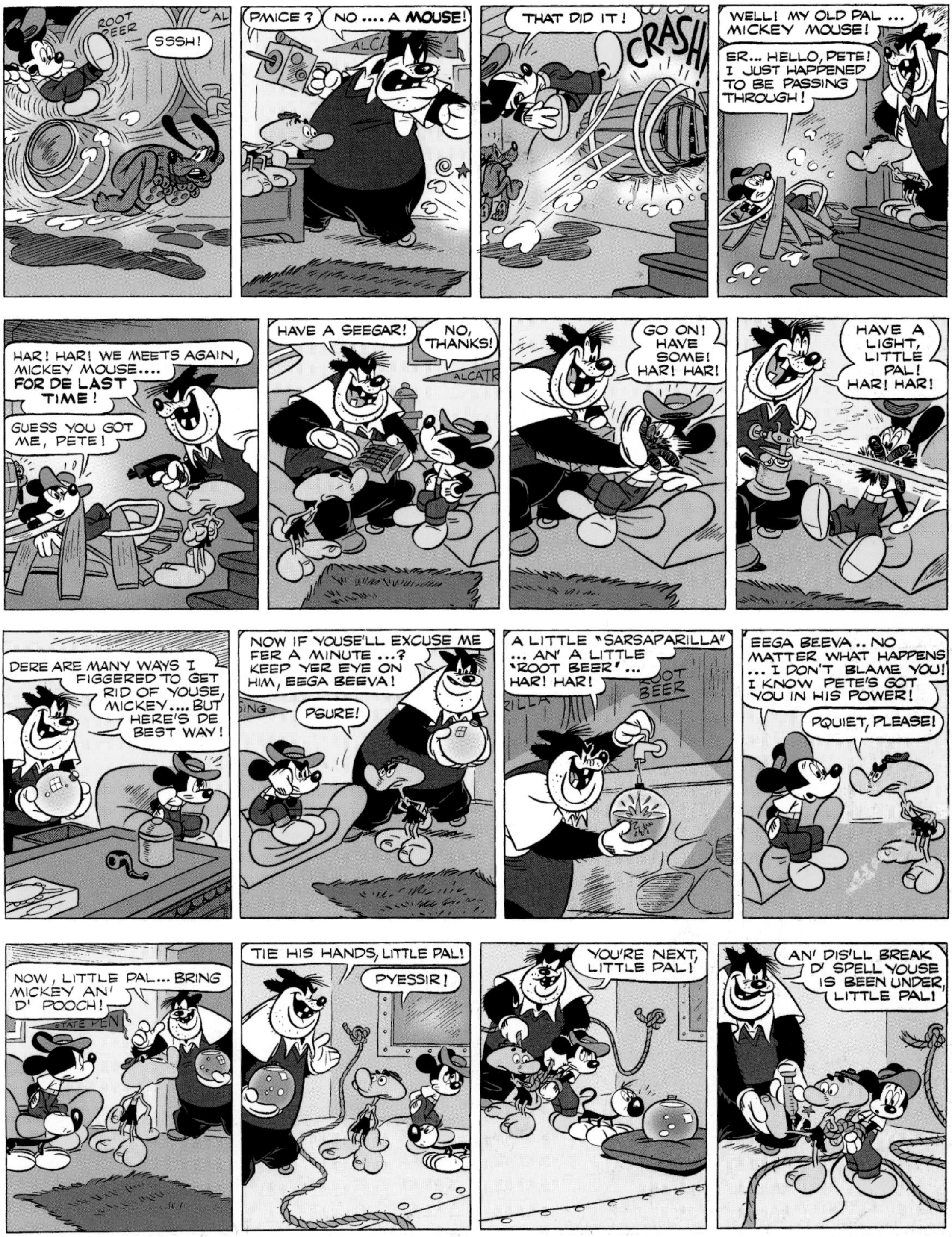
ROOT BEER
SSSH!
PMICE ?
NO .... A MOUSE!
THAT DID IT!
CRASH!
WELL! MY OLD PAL ... MICKEY MOUSE!
ER... HELLO, PETE! I JUST HAPPENED TO BE PASSING THROUGH!
HAR! HAR! WE MEETS AGAIN, MICKEY MOUSE.... FOR DE LAST TIME!
GUESS YOU GOT ME, PETE!
HAVE A SEEGAR!
NO, THANKS!
GO ON! HAVE SOME! HAR! HAR!
HAVE A LIGHT, LITTLE PAL! HAR! HAR!
DERE ARE MANY WAYS I FIGGERED TO GET RID OF YOUSE, MICKEY.... BUT HERE'S DE BEST WAY!
NOW IF YOUSE'LL EXCUSE ME FER A MINUTE ...? KEEP YER EYE ON HIM, EEGA BEEVA!
PSURE!
A LITTLE "SARSAPARILLA" ... AN' A LITTLE 'ROOT BEER' ... HAR! HAR!
ROOT BEER
EEGA BEEVA .. NO MATTER WHAT HAPPENS ... I DON'T BLAME YOU! I KNOW PETE'S GOT YOU IN HIS POWER!
PQUIET, PLEASE!
NOW, LITTLE PAL... BRING MICKEY AN' D' POOCH!
STATE PEN
TIE HIS HANDS, LITTLE PAL!
PYESSIR!
YOU'RE NEXT, LITTLE PAL!
AN' DIS'LL BREAK D' SPELL YOUSE IS BEEN UNDER, LITTLE PAL!

MICKEY MOUSE

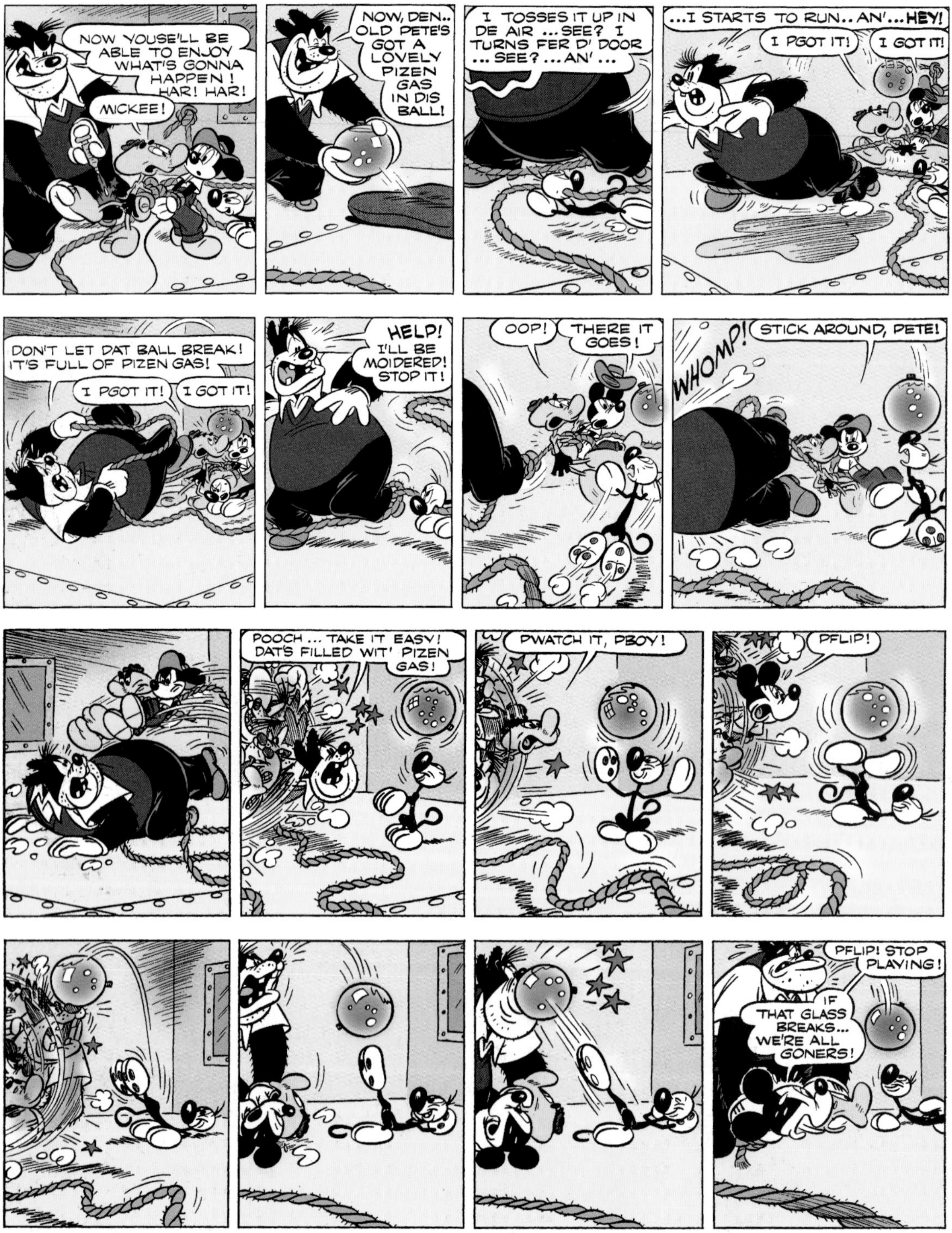
NOW YOUSE'LL BE ABLE TO ENJOY WHAT'S GONNA HAPPEN! HAR! HAR!
MICKEE!
NOW, DEN.. OLD PETE'S GOT A LOVELY PIZEN GAS IN DIS BALL!
I TOSSES IT UP IN DE AIR ... SEE? I TURNS FER D' DOOR ... SEE? ... AN' ...
...I STARTS TO RUN.. AN'...HEY!
I PGOT IT!
I GOT IT!
DON'T LET DAT BALL BREAK! IT'S FULL OF PIZEN GAS!
I PGOT IT!
I GOT IT!
HELP! I'LL BE MOIDERED! STOP IT!
OOP!
THERE IT GOES!
WHOMP!
STICK AROUND, PETE!
POOCH ... TAKE IT EASY! DAT'S FILLED WIT' PIZEN GAS!
PWATCH IT, PBOY!
PFLIP!
PFLIP! STOP PLAYING!
IF THAT GLASS BREAKS... WE'RE ALL GONERS!

PFLIP'S STRANGE POWER

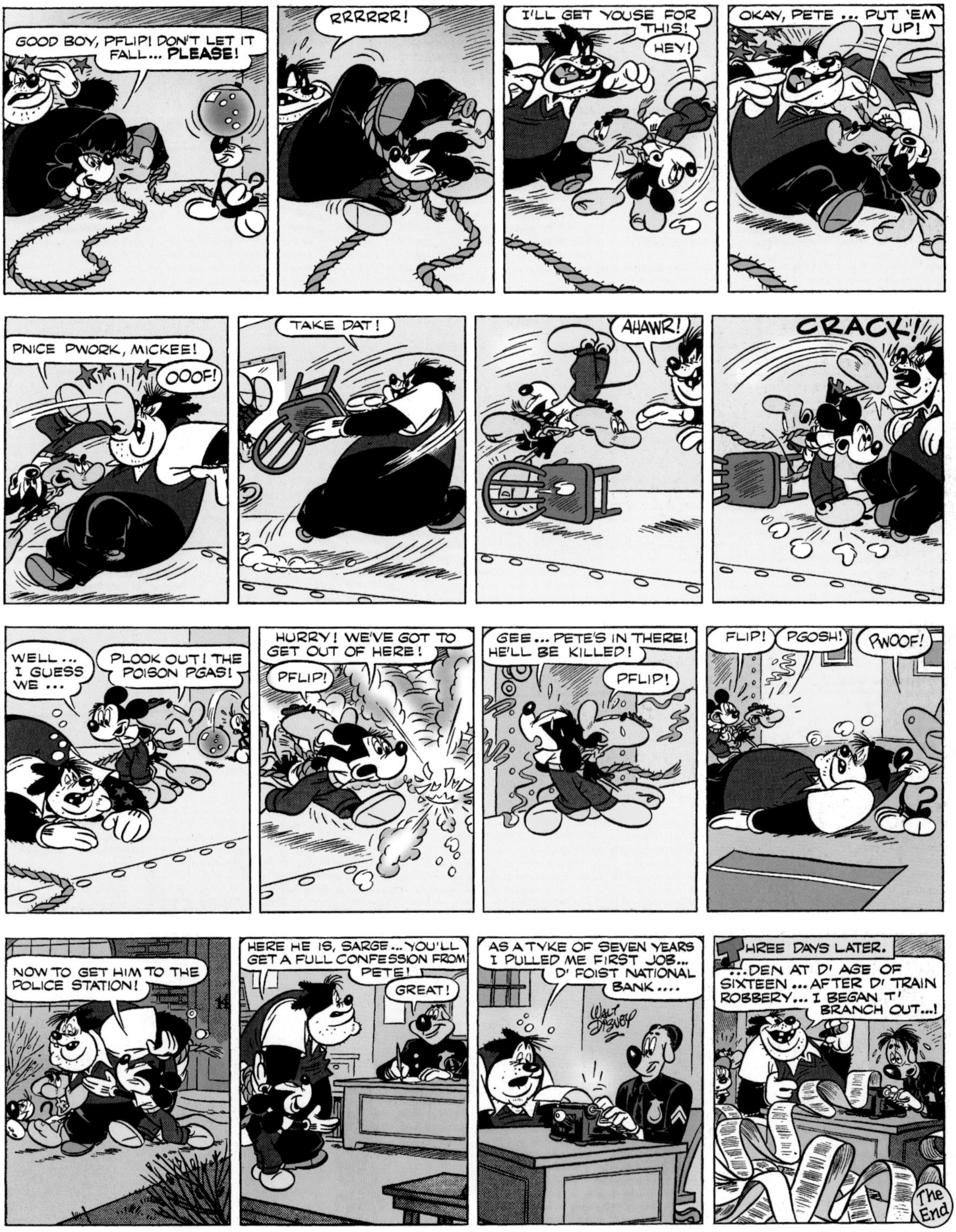
GOOD BOY, PFLIP! DON'T LET IT FALL... **PLEASE!**
RRRRRR!
I'LL GET YOUSE FOR THIS!
HEY!
OKAY, PETE ... PUT 'EM UP!
PNICE PWORK, MICKEE!
OOOF!
TAKE DAT!
AHAWR!
CRACK!
WELL ... I GUESS WE ...
PLOOK OUT! THE POISON PGAS!
HURRY! WE'VE GOT TO GET OUT OF HERE!
PFLIP!
GEE ... PETE'S IN THERE! HE'LL BE KILLED!
PFLIP!
FLIP!
PGOSH!
PWOOF!
NOW TO GET HIM TO THE POLICE STATION!
HERE HE IS, SARGE ... YOU'LL GET A FULL CONFESSION FROM PETE!
GREAT!
AS A TYKE OF SEVEN YEARS I PULLED ME FIRST JOB... D' FOIST NATIONAL BANK....
WALT DISNEY
THREE DAYS LATER.
...DEN AT D' AGE OF SIXTEEN ... AFTER D' TRAIN ROBBERY ... I BEGAN T' BRANCH OUT...!
The End

SUMMERTIME, LAZY RIVERS, HOUSEBOATS AND

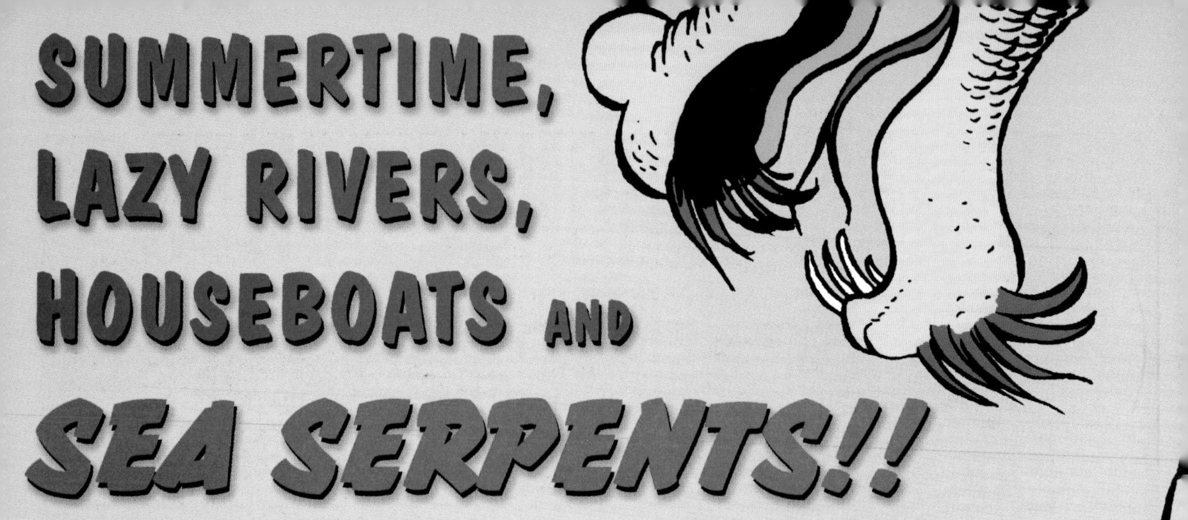

SEA SERPENTS!!

When Donald and his nephews set sail on their new houseboat for fun and adventure, their voyage is riddled with mishaps, blunders, and foul-ups... would you expect anything less from Donald? But something beyond their wildest imaginations lurks beneath the lazy waters of the Ohio River, and as usual, it's up to the nephews to crack the case!

Ride along with the ducks in Carl Barks' classic adventure, "The Terror of the River!!" in *Vacation Parade 3*, Gemstone Publishing's fun-filled collection of summertime favorites! Available at your local comic shop in May, 2006.

This year's Summer spectacular also features the wrap-around cover from the original *Vacation Parade* 3, professionally restored by Rick Keene, as well as:

- A Don Rosa pin-up page of "Terror of the River!!"
- Mickey Mouse in "Sandgate," by Noel Van Horn
- Donald and Fethry in "The Fall Guy" by Dick Kinney and Al Hubbard
- "Goofy Gives His All" by Sarah Kinney and Rodriquez
- Pluto in "The-Not-So-Still Life," by Paul Murry (from *Walt Disney's Comics and Stories* 186)
- Li'l Bad Wolf in "Fooling the Fairy," by Gil Turner (from *Walt Disney's Comics and Stories* 102)

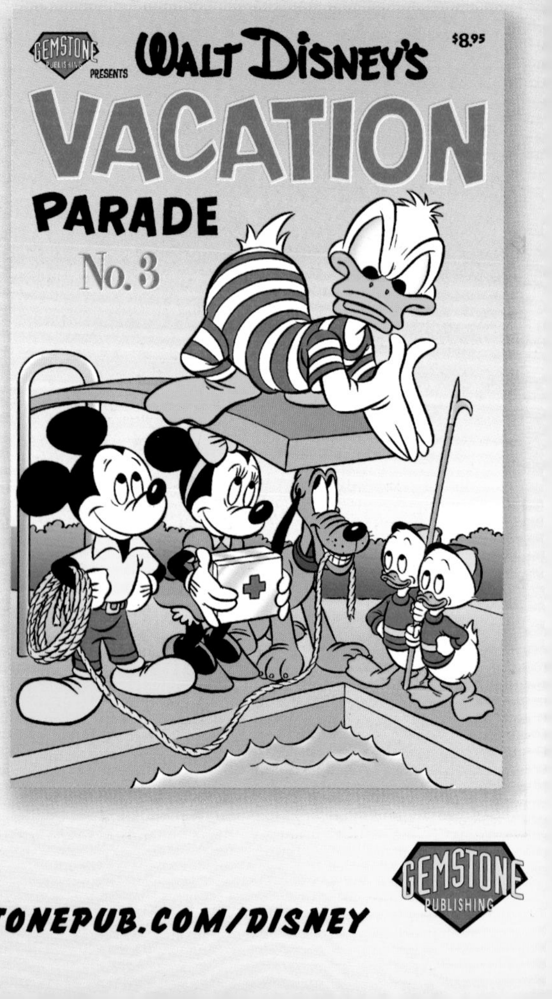
Gemstone Publishing
Presents
$8.95
Walt Disney's
VACATION PARADE
No. 3

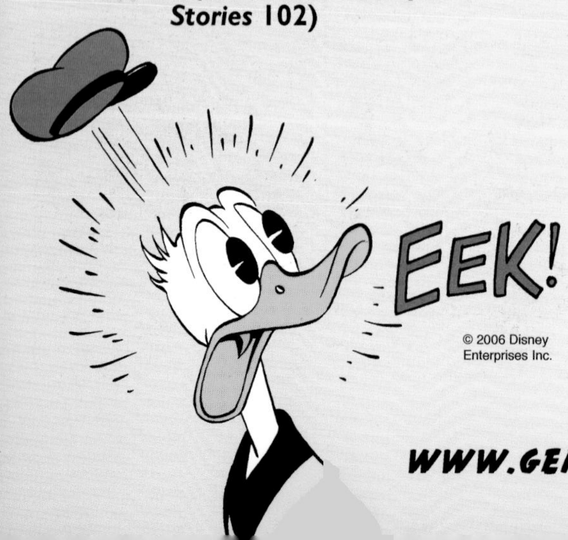
EEK!

Gemstone Publishing

WWW.GEMSTONEPUB.COM/DISNEY

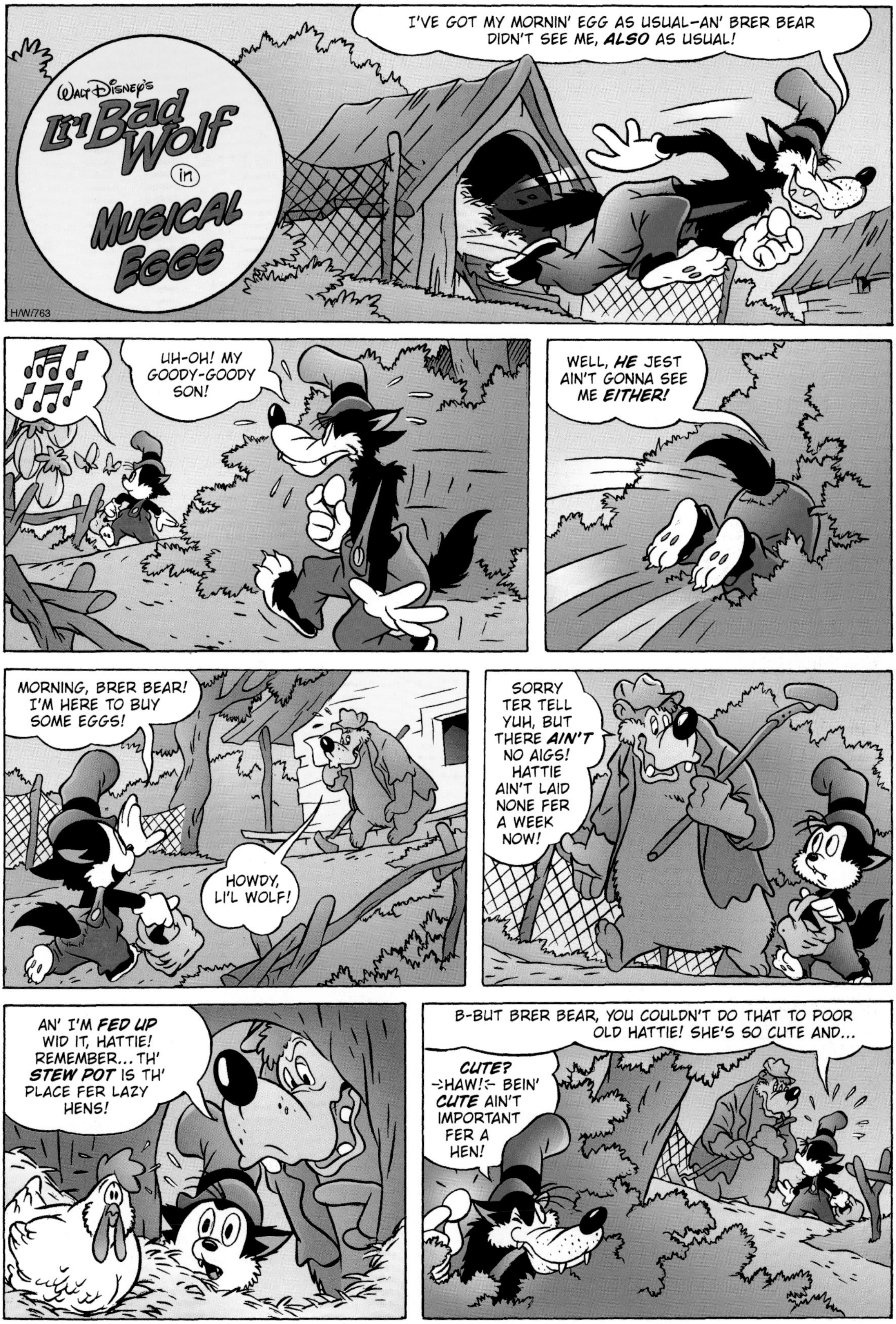

I'VE GOT MY MORNIN' EGG AS USUAL—AN' BRER BEAR DIDN'T SEE ME, ALSO AS USUAL!
WALT DISNEY'S
LI'L BAD WOLF
in
MUSICAL EGGS
H/W/763
UH-OH! MY GOODY-GOODY SON!
WELL, HE JEST AIN'T GONNA SEE ME EITHER!
MORNING, BRER BEAR! I'M HERE TO BUY SOME EGGS!
HOWDY, LI'L WOLF!
SORRY TER TELL YUH, BUT THERE AIN'T NO AIGS! HATTIE AIN'T LAID NONE FER A WEEK NOW!
AN' I'M FED UP WID IT, HATTIE! REMEMBER... TH' STEW POT IS TH' PLACE FER LAZY HENS!
B-BUT BRER BEAR, YOU COULDN'T DO THAT TO POOR OLD HATTIE! SHE'S SO CUTE AND...
CUTE? →HAW!← BEIN' CUTE AIN'T IMPORTANT FER A HEN!

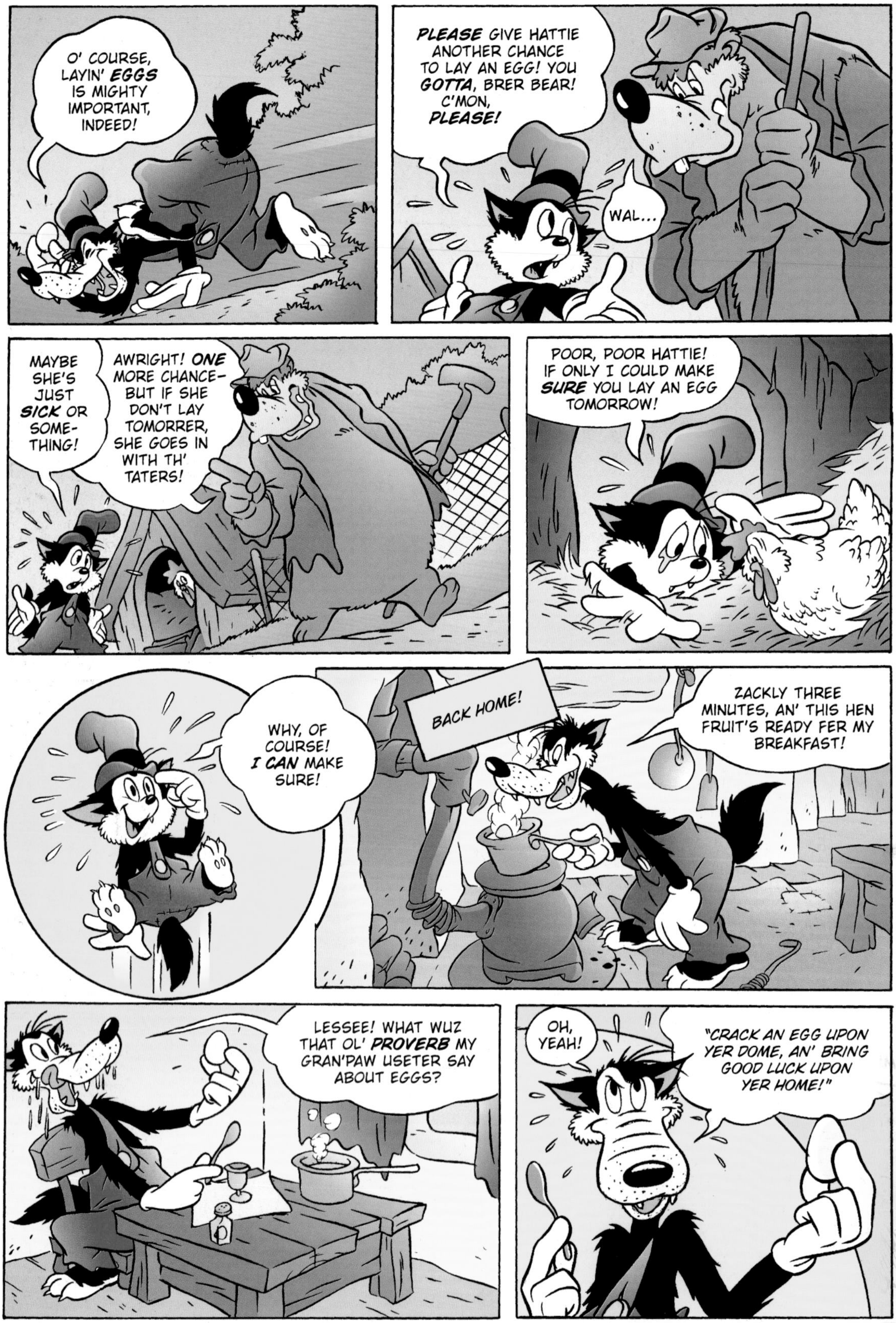
O' COURSE, LAYIN' EGGS IS MIGHTY IMPORTANT, INDEED!
PLEASE GIVE HATTIE ANOTHER CHANCE TO LAY AN EGG! YOU GOTTA, BRER BEAR! C'MON, PLEASE!
WAL...
MAYBE SHE'S JUST SICK OR SOME-THING!
AWRIGHT! ONE MORE CHANCE-BUT IF SHE DON'T LAY TOMORRER, SHE GOES IN WITH TH' TATERS!
POOR, POOR HATTIE! IF ONLY I COULD MAKE SURE YOU LAY AN EGG TOMORROW!
WHY, OF COURSE! I CAN MAKE SURE!
BACK HOME!
ZACKLY THREE MINUTES, AN' THIS HEN FRUIT'S READY FER MY BREAKFAST!
LESSEE! WHAT WUZ THAT OL' PROVERB MY GRAN'PAW USETER SAY ABOUT EGGS?
OH, YEAH!
"CRACK AN EGG UPON YER DOME, AN' BRING GOOD LUCK UPON YER HOME!"

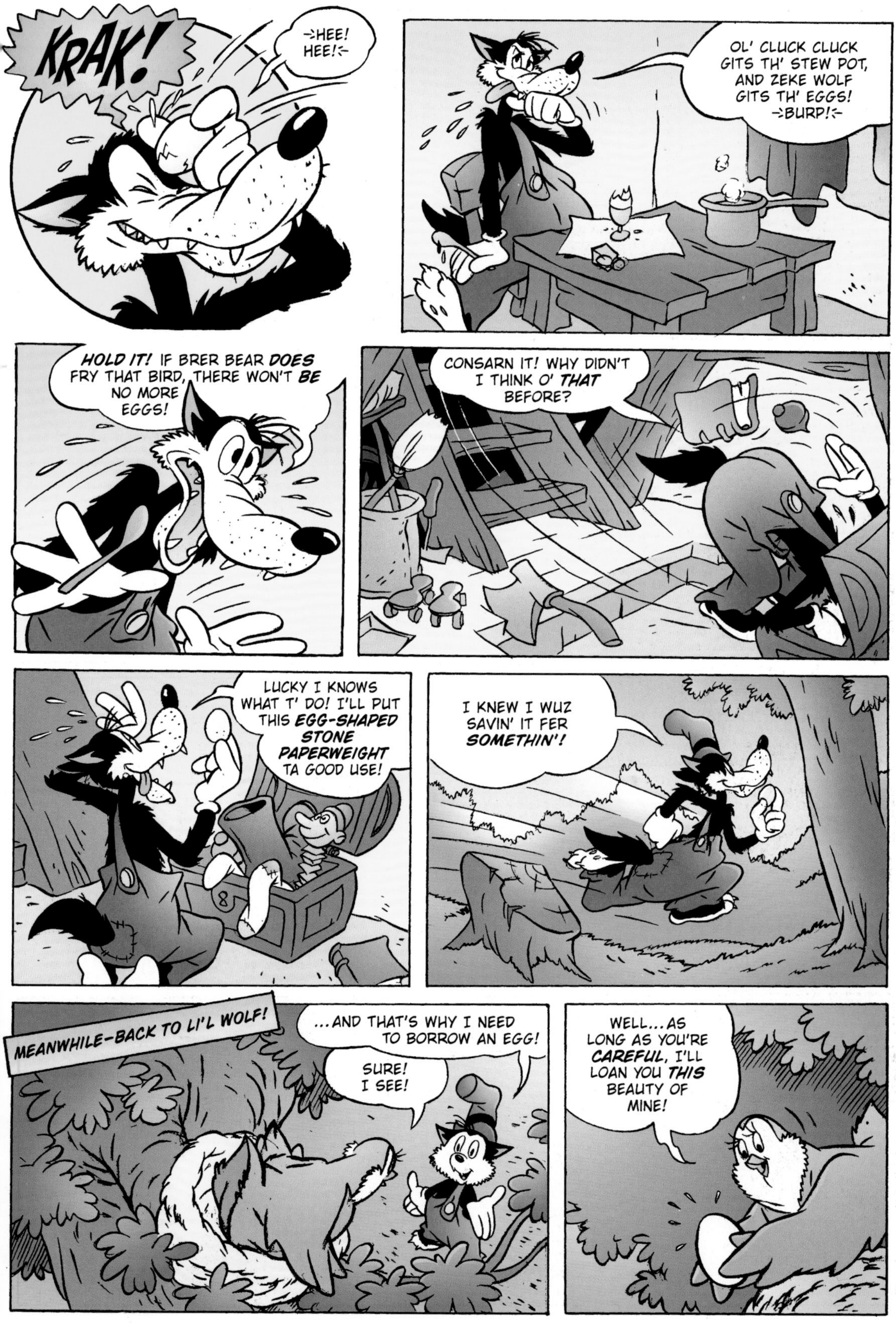
KRAK!
-HEE! HEE!-
OL' CLUCK CLUCK GITS TH' STEW POT, AND ZEKE WOLF GITS TH' EGGS! -BURP!-
HOLD IT! IF BRER BEAR DOES FRY THAT BIRD, THERE WON'T BE NO MORE EGGS!
CONSARN IT! WHY DIDN'T I THINK O' THAT BEFORE?
LUCKY I KNOWS WHAT T' DO! I'LL PUT THIS EGG-SHAPED STONE PAPERWEIGHT TA GOOD USE!
I KNEW I WUZ SAVIN' IT FER SOMETHIN'!
MEANWHILE—BACK TO LI'L WOLF!
...AND THAT'S WHY I NEED TO BORROW AN EGG!
SURE! I SEE!
WELL... AS LONG AS YOU'RE CAREFUL, I'LL LOAN YOU THIS BEAUTY OF MINE!

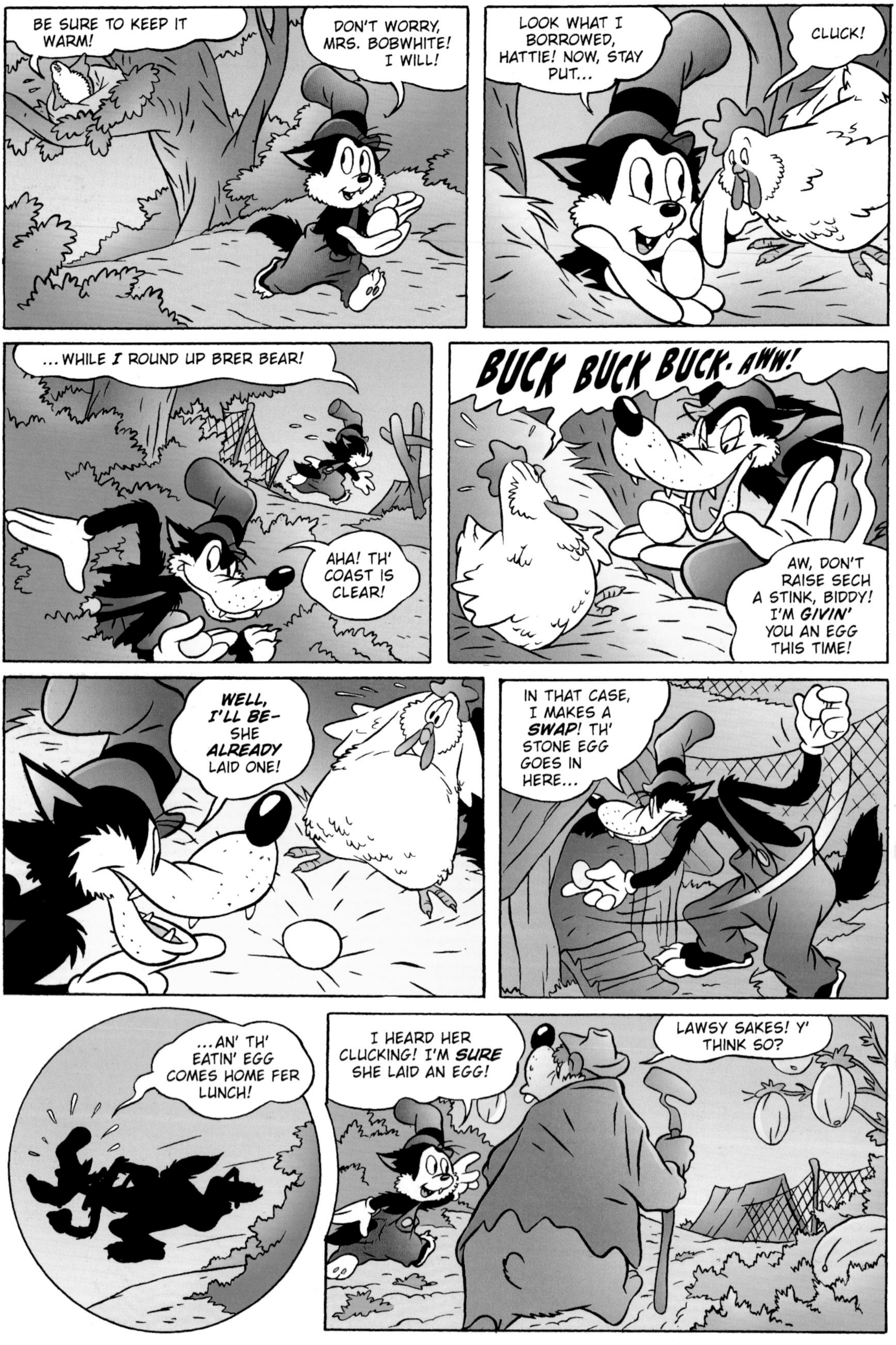
BE SURE TO KEEP IT WARM!
DON'T WORRY, MRS. BOBWHITE! I WILL!
LOOK WHAT I BORROWED, HATTIE! NOW, STAY PUT...
CLUCK!
...WHILE I ROUND UP BRER BEAR!
AHA! TH' COAST IS CLEAR!
BUCK BUCK BUCK- AWW!
AW, DON'T RAISE SECH A STINK, BIDDY! I'M GIVIN' YOU AN EGG THIS TIME!
WELL, I'LL BE- SHE ALREADY LAID ONE!
IN THAT CASE, I MAKES A SWAP! TH' STONE EGG GOES IN HERE...
...AN' TH' EATIN' EGG COMES HOME FER LUNCH!
I HEARD HER CLUCKING! I'M SURE SHE LAID AN EGG!
LAWSY SAKES! Y' THINK SO?

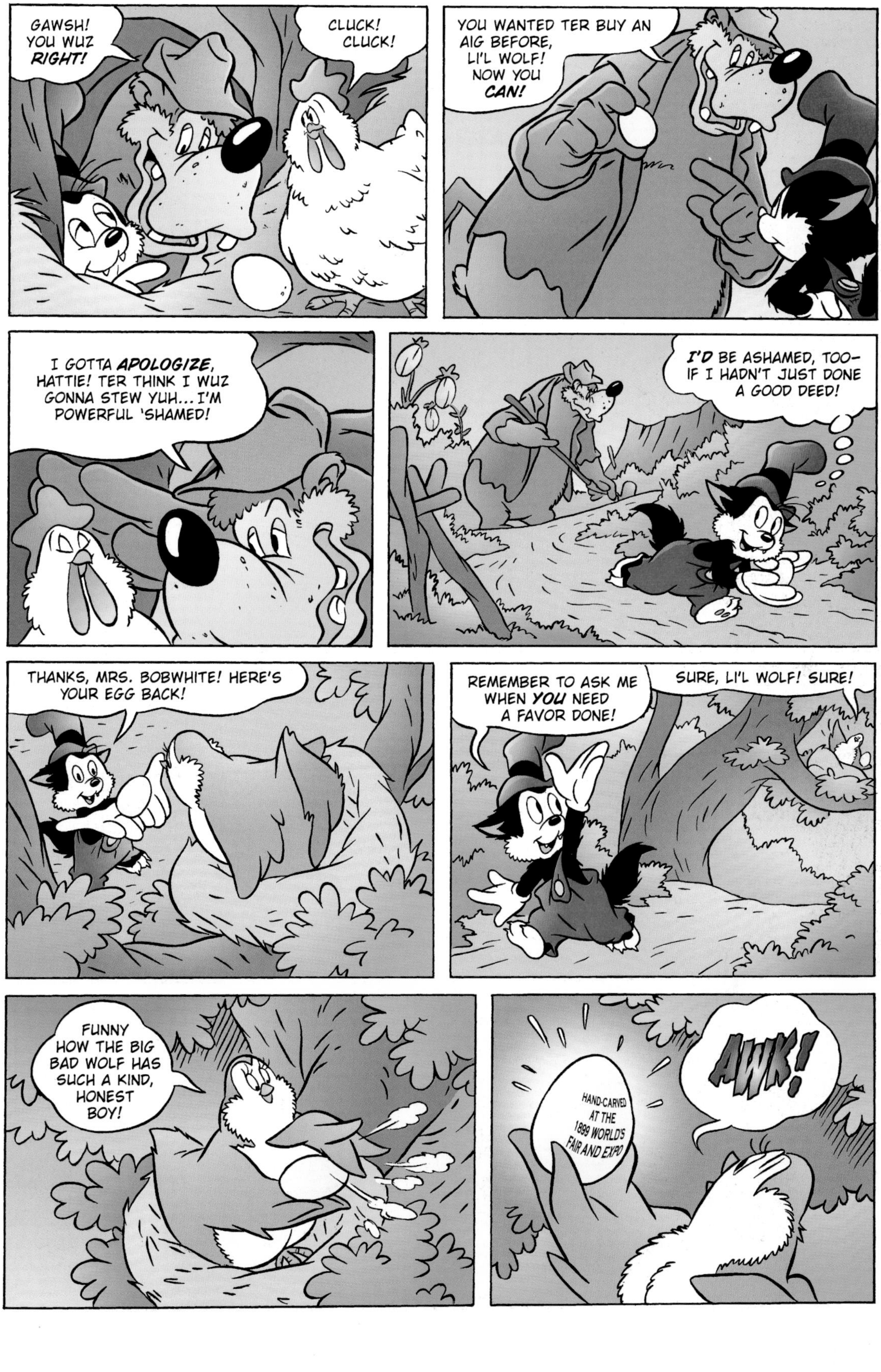
GAWSH! YOU WUZ RIGHT!
CLUCK! CLUCK!
YOU WANTED TER BUY AN AIG BEFORE, LI'L WOLF! NOW YOU CAN!
I GOTTA APOLOGIZE, HATTIE! TER THINK I WUZ GONNA STEW YUH... I'M POWERFUL 'SHAMED!
I'D BE ASHAMED, TOO— IF I HADN'T JUST DONE A GOOD DEED!
THANKS, MRS. BOBWHITE! HERE'S YOUR EGG BACK!
REMEMBER TO ASK ME WHEN YOU NEED A FAVOR DONE!
SURE, LI'L WOLF! SURE!
FUNNY HOW THE BIG BAD WOLF HAS SUCH A KIND, HONEST BOY!
HAND-CARVED AT THE 1899 WORLD'S FAIR AND EXPO
AWK!

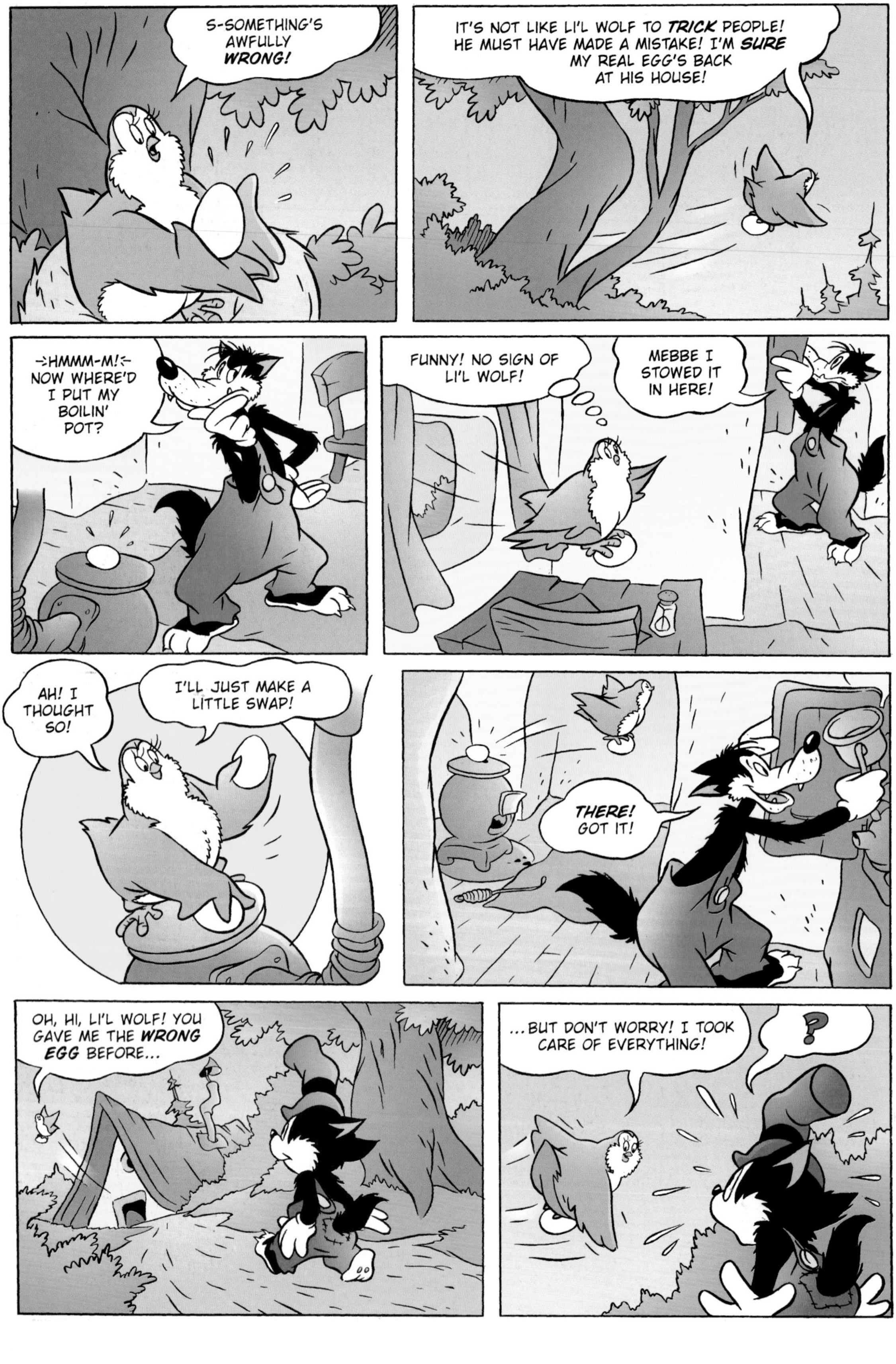
S-SOMETHING'S AWFULLY WRONG!
IT'S NOT LIKE LI'L WOLF TO TRICK PEOPLE! HE MUST HAVE MADE A MISTAKE! I'M SURE MY REAL EGG'S BACK AT HIS HOUSE!
HMMM-M! NOW WHERE'D I PUT MY BOILIN' POT?
FUNNY! NO SIGN OF LI'L WOLF!
MEBBE I STOWED IT IN HERE!
AH! I THOUGHT SO!
I'LL JUST MAKE A LITTLE SWAP!
THERE! GOT IT!
OH, HI, LI'L WOLF! YOU GAVE ME THE WRONG EGG BEFORE...
...BUT DON'T WORRY! I TOOK CARE OF EVERYTHING!
?

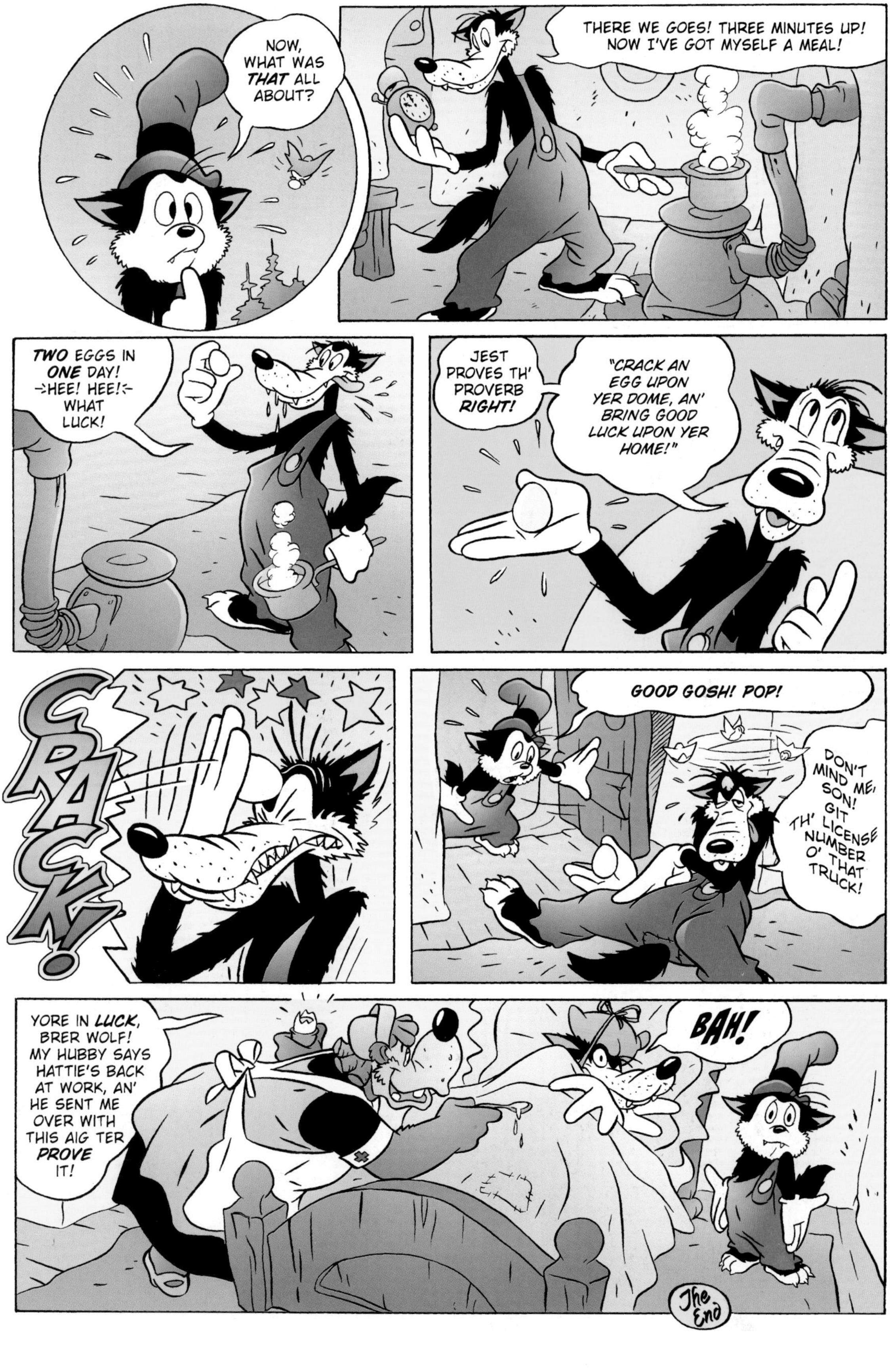
NOW, WHAT WAS *THAT* ALL ABOUT?
THERE WE GOES! THREE MINUTES UP! NOW I'VE GOT MYSELF A MEAL!
TWO EGGS IN *ONE* DAY! -HEE! HEE!- WHAT LUCK!
JEST PROVES TH' PROVERB *RIGHT!*
"CRACK AN EGG UPON YER DOME, AN' BRING GOOD LUCK UPON YER HOME!"
CRACK!
GOOD GOSH! POP!
DON'T MIND ME, SON! GIT TH' LICENSE NUMBER O' THAT TRUCK!
YORE IN *LUCK*, BRER WOLF! MY HUBBY SAYS HATTIE'S BACK AT WORK, AN' HE SENT ME OVER WITH THIS AIG TER *PROVE* IT!
BAH!
The End

FREE COMIC BOOK DAY

SATURDAY
MAY 6, 2006

www.freecomicbookday.com

TM

ASK ABOUT YOUR FREE COMIC BOOK!

At Participating Retailers Only

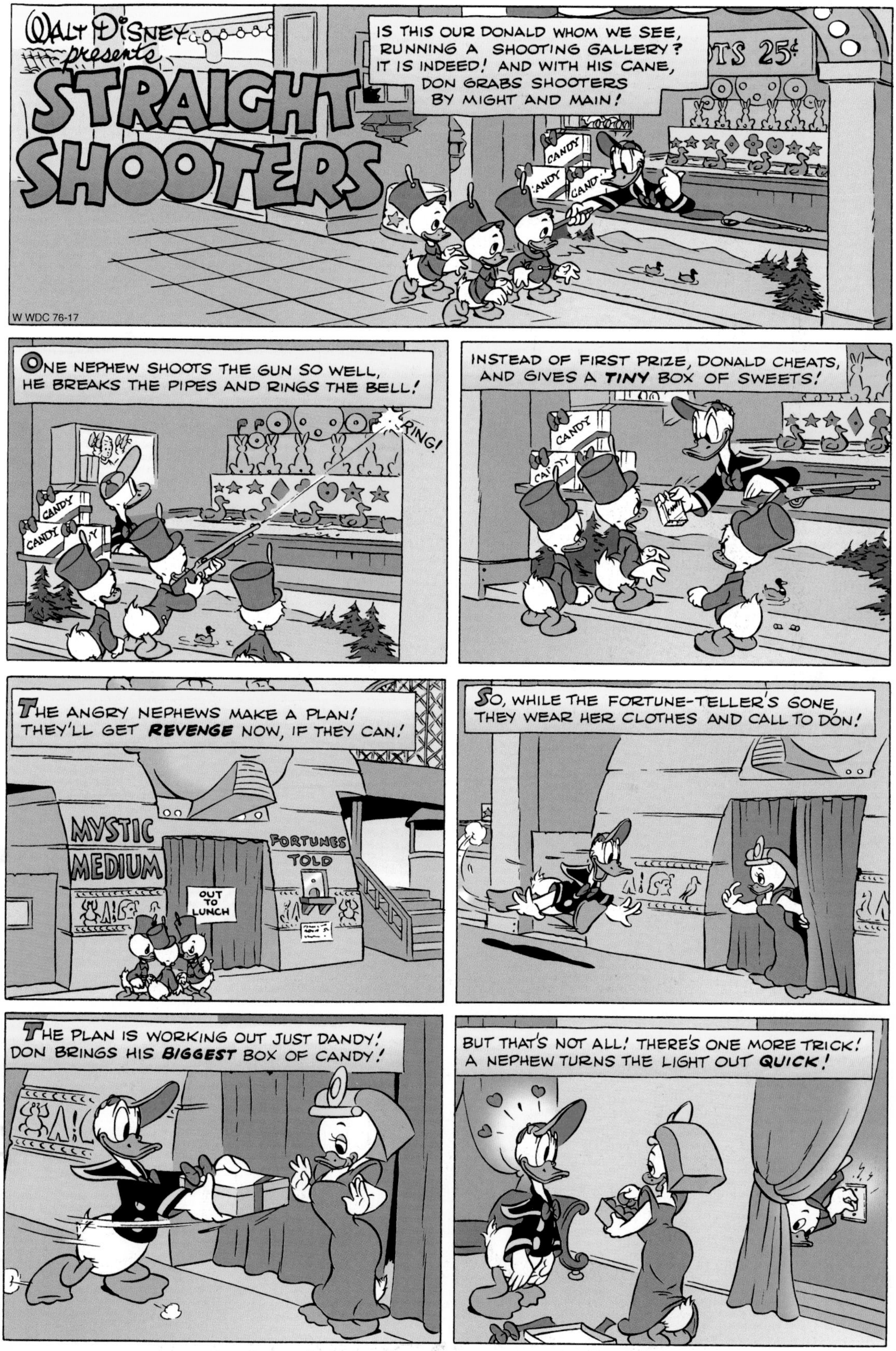
WALT DISNEY presents
STRAIGHT SHOOTERS
IS THIS OUR DONALD WHOM WE SEE, RUNNING A SHOOTING GALLERY? IT IS INDEED! AND WITH HIS CANE, DON GRABS SHOOTERS BY MIGHT AND MAIN!
W WDC 76-17
ONE NEPHEW SHOOTS THE GUN SO WELL, HE BREAKS THE PIPES AND RINGS THE BELL!
RING!
INSTEAD OF FIRST PRIZE, DONALD CHEATS, AND GIVES A TINY BOX OF SWEETS!
THE ANGRY NEPHEWS MAKE A PLAN! THEY'LL GET REVENGE NOW, IF THEY CAN!
MYSTIC MEDIUM
FORTUNES TOLD
OUT TO LUNCH
SO, WHILE THE FORTUNE-TELLER'S GONE, THEY WEAR HER CLOTHES AND CALL TO DON!
THE PLAN IS WORKING OUT JUST DANDY! DON BRINGS HIS BIGGEST BOX OF CANDY!
BUT THAT'S NOT ALL! THERE'S ONE MORE TRICK! A NEPHEW TURNS THE LIGHT OUT QUICK!

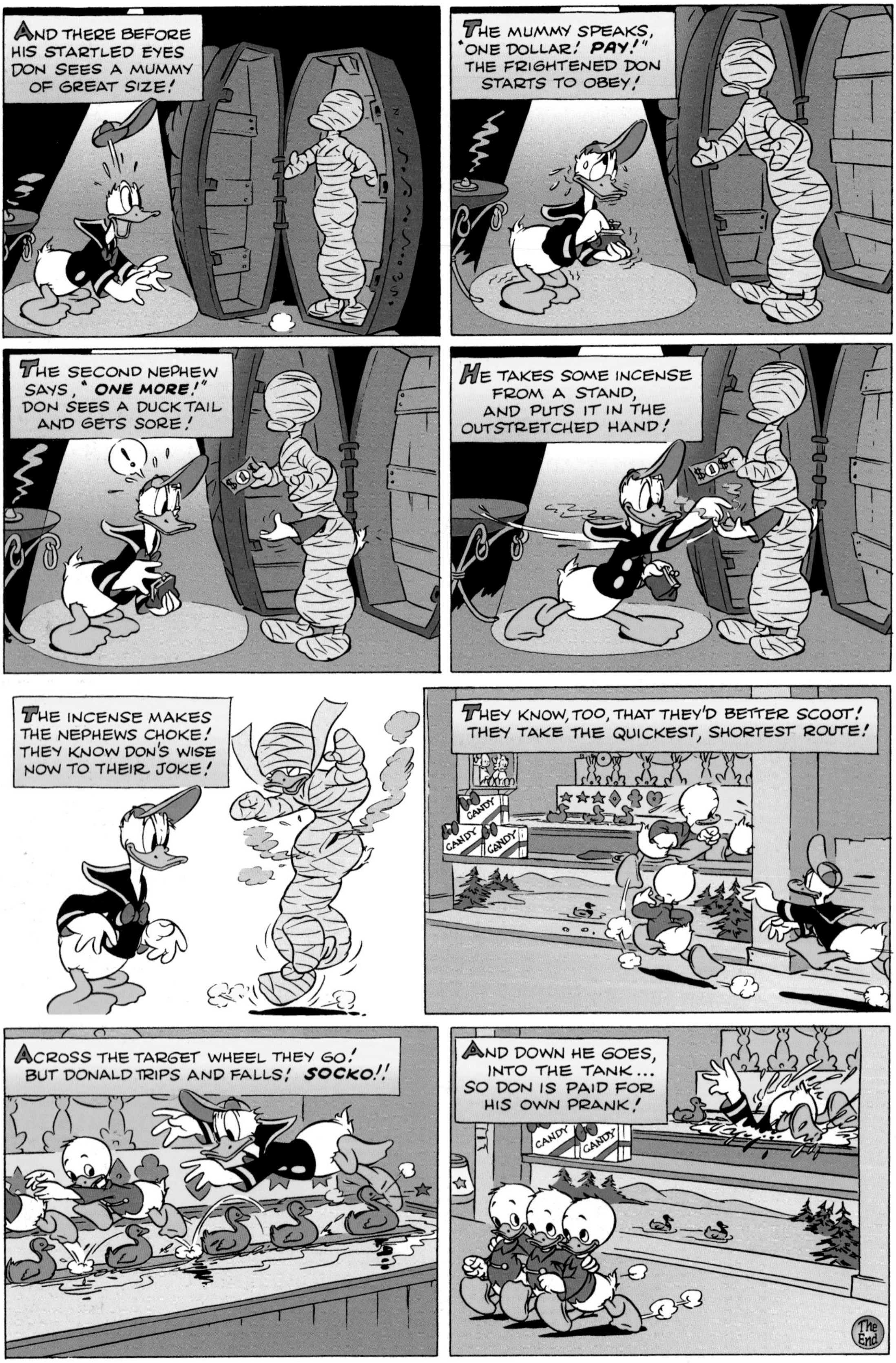
AND THERE BEFORE HIS STARTLED EYES DON SEES A MUMMY OF GREAT SIZE!
THE MUMMY SPEAKS, "ONE DOLLAR! PAY!" THE FRIGHTENED DON STARTS TO OBEY!
THE SECOND NEPHEW SAYS, "ONE MORE!" DON SEES A DUCK TAIL AND GETS SORE!
!
HE TAKES SOME INCENSE FROM A STAND, AND PUTS IT IN THE OUTSTRETCHED HAND!
THE INCENSE MAKES THE NEPHEWS CHOKE! THEY KNOW DON'S WISE NOW TO THEIR JOKE!
THEY KNOW, TOO, THAT THEY'D BETTER SCOOT! THEY TAKE THE QUICKEST, SHORTEST ROUTE!
CANDY
CANDY
CANDY
ACROSS THE TARGET WHEEL THEY GO! BUT DONALD TRIPS AND FALLS! SOCKO!!
AND DOWN HE GOES, INTO THE TANK... SO DON IS PAID FOR HIS OWN PRANK!
CANDY
CANDY
The End

Walt Disney's GOOFY in ESTEEM FOR A DAY

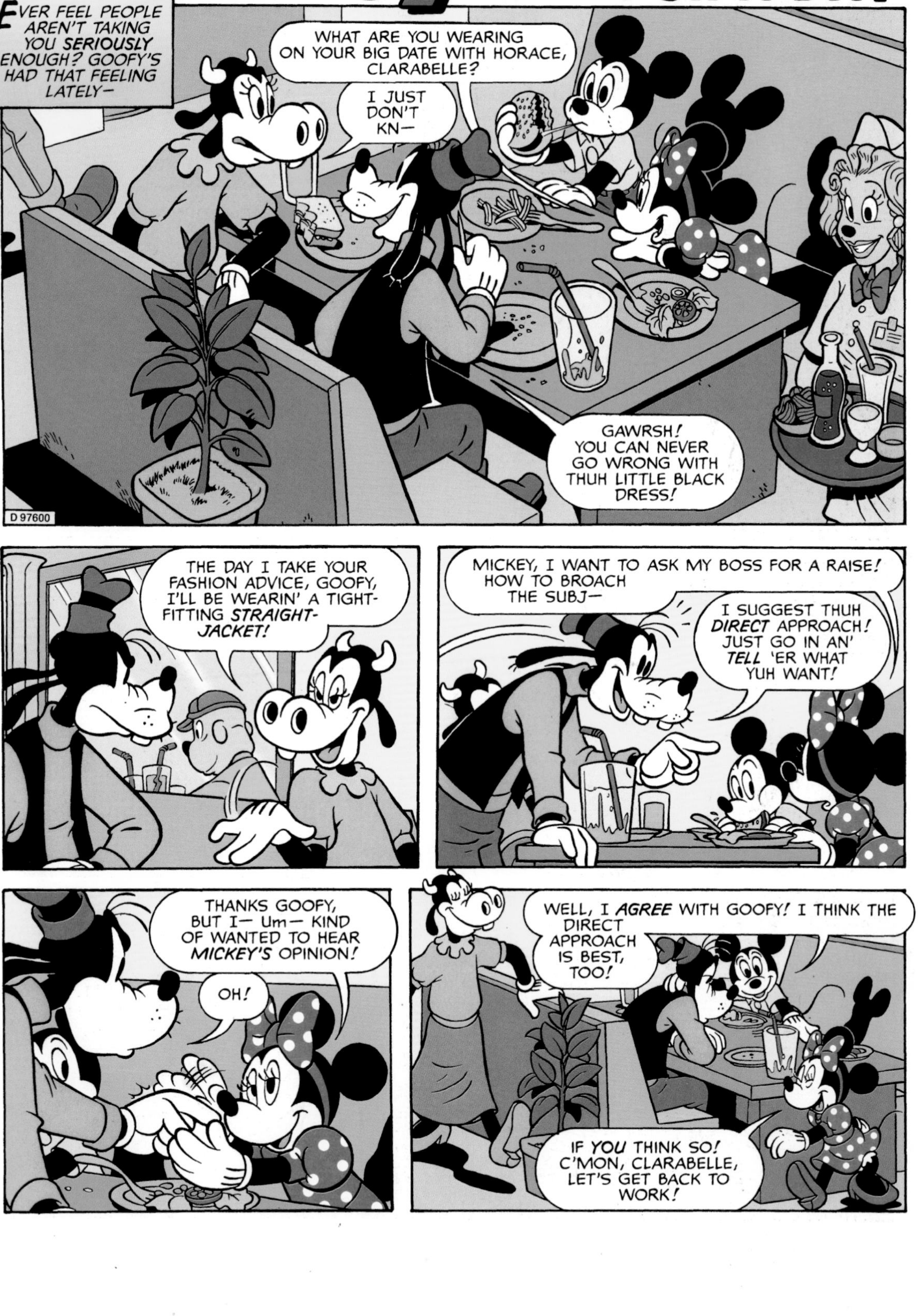

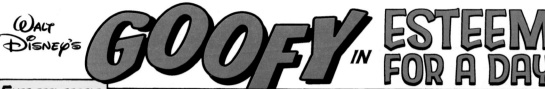

EVER FEEL PEOPLE AREN'T TAKING YOU SERIOUSLY ENOUGH? GOOFY'S HAD THAT FEELING LATELY—
WHAT ARE YOU WEARING ON YOUR BIG DATE WITH HORACE, CLARABELLE?
I JUST DON'T KN—
GAWRSH! YOU CAN NEVER GO WRONG WITH THUH LITTLE BLACK DRESS!
D 97600
THE DAY I TAKE YOUR FASHION ADVICE, GOOFY, I'LL BE WEARIN' A TIGHT-FITTING STRAIGHT-JACKET!
MICKEY, I WANT TO ASK MY BOSS FOR A RAISE! HOW TO BROACH THE SUBJ—
I SUGGEST THUH DIRECT APPROACH! JUST GO IN AN' TELL 'ER WHAT YUH WANT!
THANKS GOOFY, BUT I— Um— KIND OF WANTED TO HEAR MICKEY'S OPINION!
OH!
WELL, I AGREE WITH GOOFY! I THINK THE DIRECT APPROACH IS BEST, TOO!
IF YOU THINK SO! C'MON, CLARABELLE, LET'S GET BACK TO WORK!

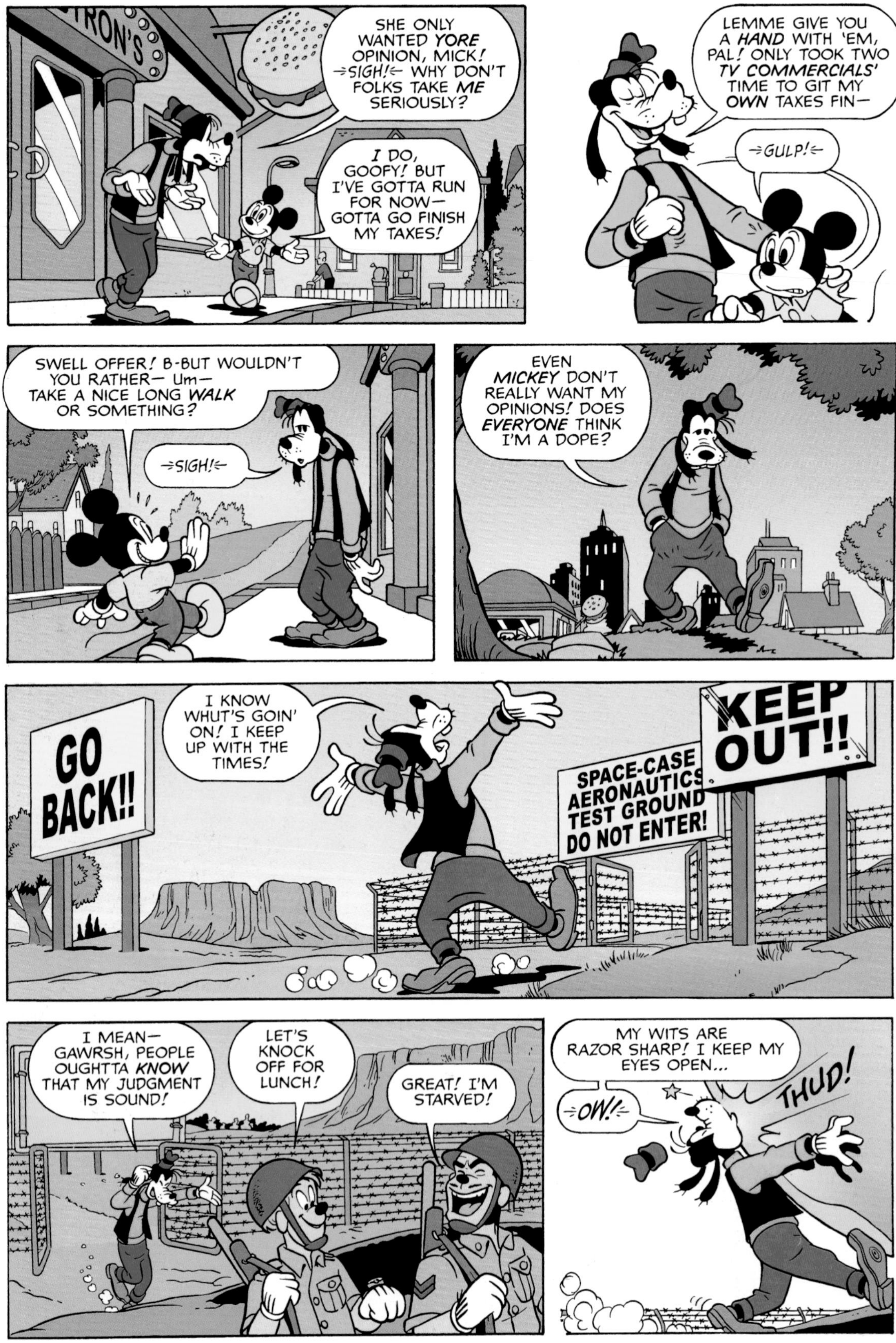
TRON'S
SHE ONLY WANTED YORE OPINION, MICK! ⇒SIGH!⇐ WHY DON'T FOLKS TAKE ME SERIOUSLY?
I DO, GOOFY! BUT I'VE GOTTA RUN FOR NOW— GOTTA GO FINISH MY TAXES!
LEMME GIVE YOU A HAND WITH 'EM, PAL! ONLY TOOK TWO TV COMMERCIALS' TIME TO GIT MY OWN TAXES FIN—
⇒GULP!⇐
SWELL OFFER! B-BUT WOULDN'T YOU RATHER— Um— TAKE A NICE LONG WALK OR SOMETHING?
⇒SIGH!⇐
EVEN MICKEY DON'T REALLY WANT MY OPINIONS! DOES EVERYONE THINK I'M A DOPE?
GO BACK!!
I KNOW WHUT'S GOIN' ON! I KEEP UP WITH THE TIMES!
SPACE-CASE AERONAUTICS TEST GROUND DO NOT ENTER!
KEEP OUT!!
I MEAN— GAWRSH, PEOPLE OUGHTTA KNOW THAT MY JUDGMENT IS SOUND!
LET'S KNOCK OFF FOR LUNCH!
GREAT! I'M STARVED!
MY WITS ARE RAZOR SHARP! I KEEP MY EYES OPEN...
⇒OW!⇐
THUD!

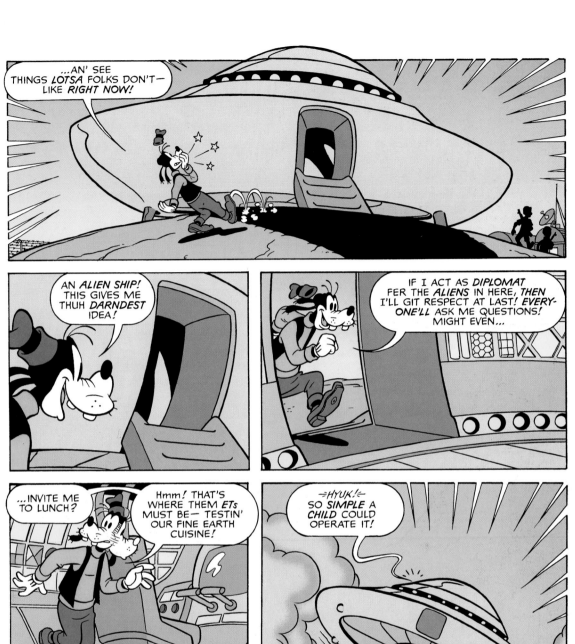

...AN' SEE THINGS *LOTSA* FOLKS DON'T— LIKE *RIGHT NOW!*

AN *ALIEN SHIP!* THIS GIVES ME THUH *DARNDEST* IDEA!

IF I ACT AS *DIPLOMAT* FER THE *ALIENS* IN HERE, *THEN* I'LL GIT RESPECT AT LAST! *EVERY-ONE'LL* ASK ME QUESTIONS! MIGHT EVEN...

...INVITE ME TO LUNCH?

Hmm! THAT'S WHERE THEM *ETs* MUST BE— TESTIN' OUR FINE EARTH CUISINE!

I'LL *PARK* THEIR SAUCER BETTER SO'S IT AIN'T IN FOLKS' WAY! THEY'LL *LOVE* ME FER THAT!

WARP | TAKE OFF

~HYUK!~ SO *SIMPLE* A *CHILD* COULD OPERATE IT!

ROAR!

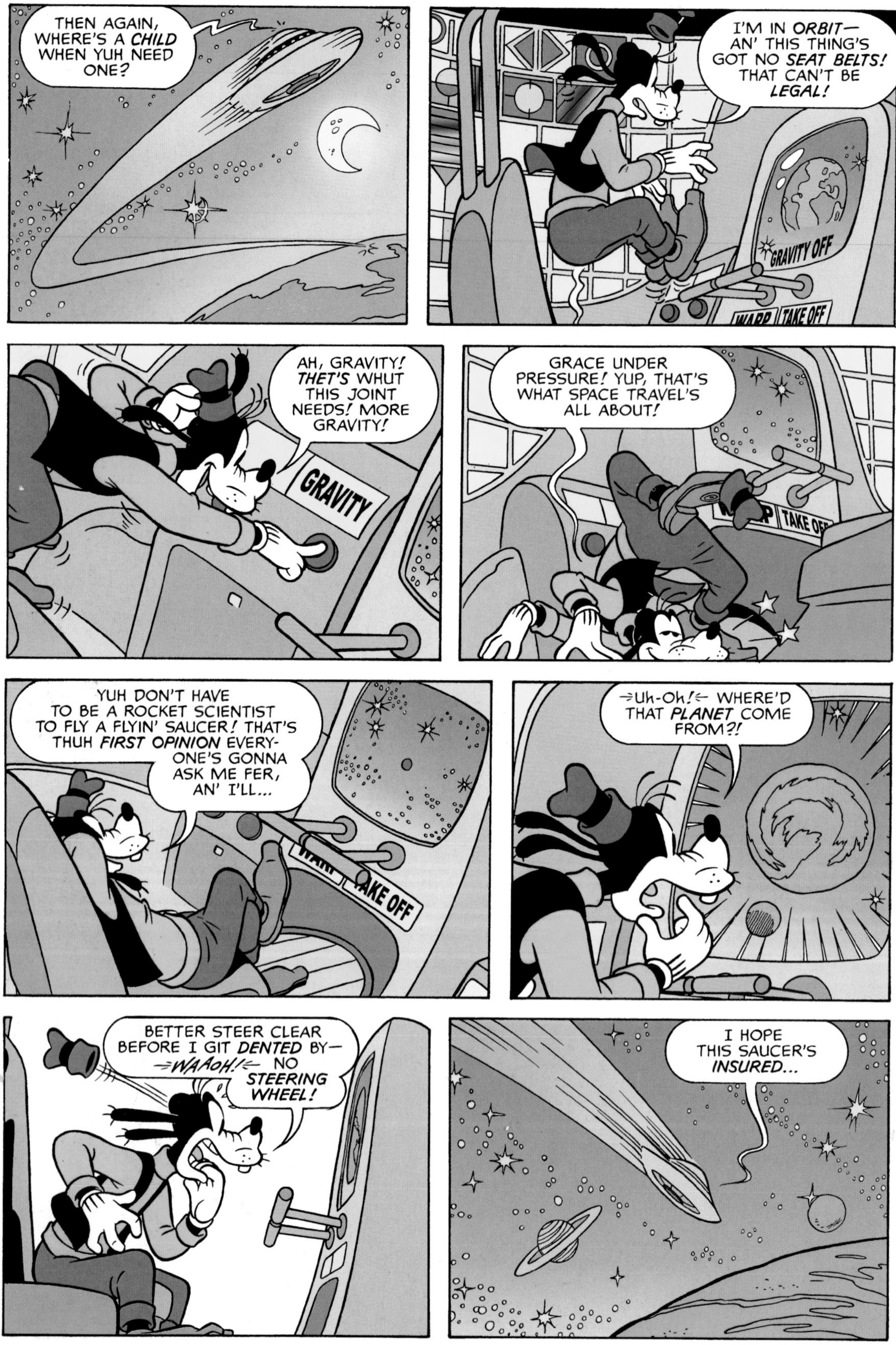
THEN AGAIN, WHERE'S A CHILD WHEN YUH NEED ONE?
I'M IN ORBIT— AN' THIS THING'S GOT NO SEAT BELTS! THAT CAN'T BE LEGAL!
GRAVITY OFF
WARP
TAKE OFF
AH, GRAVITY! THET'S WHUT THIS JOINT NEEDS! MORE GRAVITY!
GRAVITY
GRACE UNDER PRESSURE! YUP, THAT'S WHAT SPACE TRAVEL'S ALL ABOUT!
TAKE OFF
YUH DON'T HAVE TO BE A ROCKET SCIENTIST TO FLY A FLYIN' SAUCER! THAT'S THUH FIRST OPINION EVERY-ONE'S GONNA ASK ME FER, AN' I'LL...
TAKE OFF
Uh-Oh! WHERE'D THAT PLANET COME FROM?!
BETTER STEER CLEAR BEFORE I GIT DENTED BY— WAAOH! NO STEERING WHEEL!
I HOPE THIS SAUCER'S INSURED...

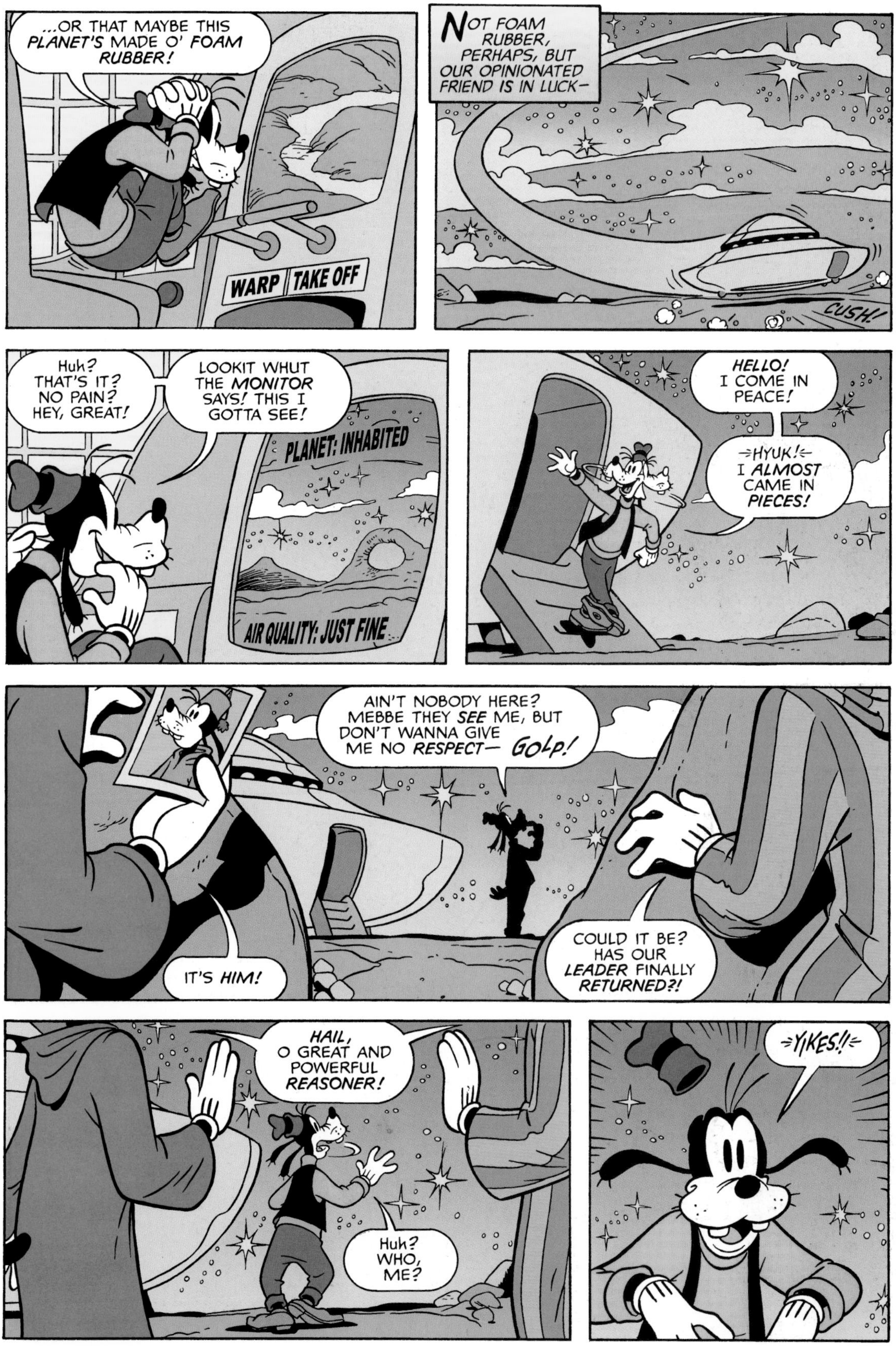
...OR THAT MAYBE THIS PLANET'S MADE O' FOAM RUBBER!
WARP
TAKE OFF
NOT FOAM RUBBER, PERHAPS, BUT OUR OPINIONATED FRIEND IS IN LUCK—
CUSH!
Huh? THAT'S IT? NO PAIN? HEY, GREAT!
LOOKIT WHUT THE MONITOR SAYS! THIS I GOTTA SEE!
PLANET: INHABITED
AIR QUALITY: JUST FINE
HELLO! I COME IN PEACE!
HYUK! I ALMOST CAME IN PIECES!
AIN'T NOBODY HERE? MEBBE THEY SEE ME, BUT DON'T WANNA GIVE ME NO RESPECT— GOLP!
IT'S HIM!
COULD IT BE? HAS OUR LEADER FINALLY RETURNED?!
HAIL, O GREAT AND POWERFUL REASONER!
Huh? WHO, ME?
YIKES!!

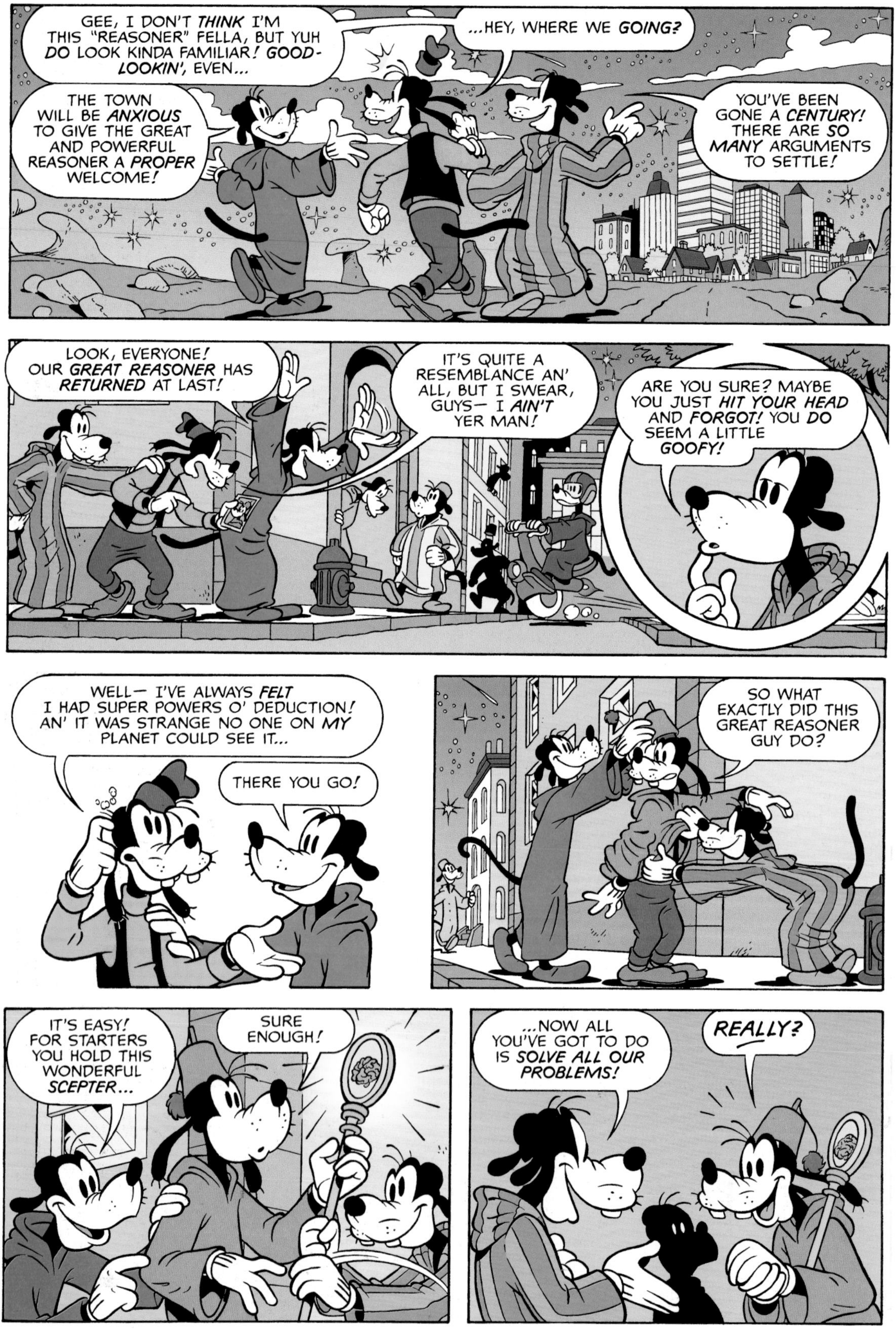
GEE, I DON'T THINK I'M THIS "REASONER" FELLA, BUT YUH DO LOOK KINDA FAMILIAR! GOOD-LOOKIN', EVEN...
...HEY, WHERE WE GOING?
THE TOWN WILL BE ANXIOUS TO GIVE THE GREAT AND POWERFUL REASONER A PROPER WELCOME!
YOU'VE BEEN GONE A CENTURY! THERE ARE SO MANY ARGUMENTS TO SETTLE!
LOOK, EVERYONE! OUR GREAT REASONER HAS RETURNED AT LAST!
IT'S QUITE A RESEMBLANCE AN' ALL, BUT I SWEAR, GUYS— I AIN'T YER MAN!
ARE YOU SURE? MAYBE YOU JUST HIT YOUR HEAD AND FORGOT! YOU DO SEEM A LITTLE GOOFY!
WELL— I'VE ALWAYS FELT I HAD SUPER POWERS O' DEDUCTION! AN' IT WAS STRANGE NO ONE ON MY PLANET COULD SEE IT...
THERE YOU GO!
SO WHAT EXACTLY DID THIS GREAT REASONER GUY DO?
IT'S EASY! FOR STARTERS YOU HOLD THIS WONDERFUL SCEPTER...
SURE ENOUGH!
...NOW ALL YOU'VE GOT TO DO IS SOLVE ALL OUR PROBLEMS!
REALLY?

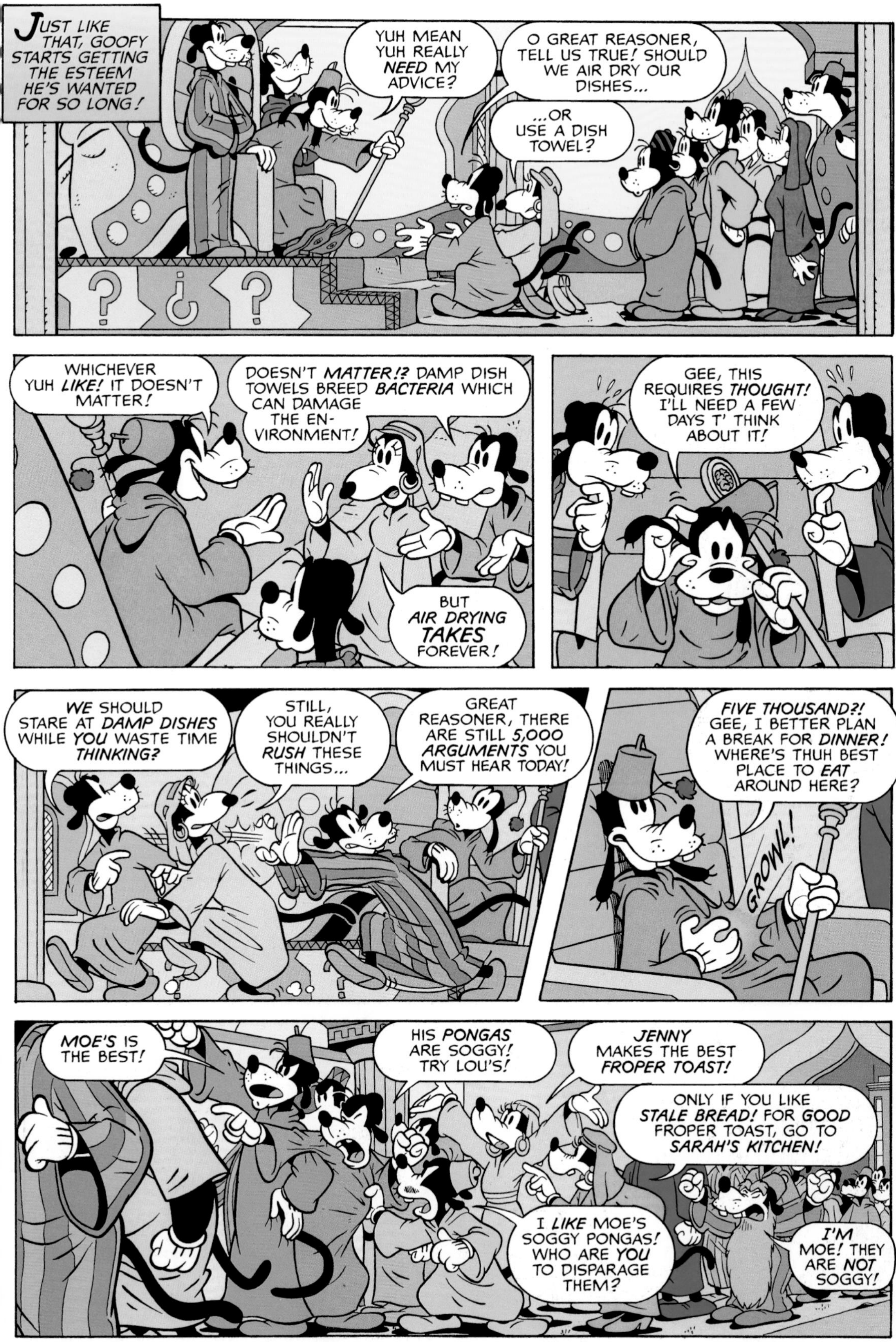
JUST LIKE THAT, GOOFY STARTS GETTING THE ESTEEM HE'S WANTED FOR SO LONG!
YUH MEAN YUH REALLY NEED MY ADVICE?
O GREAT REASONER, TELL US TRUE! SHOULD WE AIR DRY OUR DISHES...
...OR USE A DISH TOWEL?
WHICHEVER YUH LIKE! IT DOESN'T MATTER!
DOESN'T MATTER!? DAMP DISH TOWELS BREED BACTERIA WHICH CAN DAMAGE THE EN-VIRONMENT!
BUT AIR DRYING TAKES FOREVER!
GEE, THIS REQUIRES THOUGHT! I'LL NEED A FEW DAYS T' THINK ABOUT IT!
WE SHOULD STARE AT DAMP DISHES WHILE YOU WASTE TIME THINKING?
STILL, YOU REALLY SHOULDN'T RUSH THESE THINGS...
GREAT REASONER, THERE ARE STILL 5,000 ARGUMENTS YOU MUST HEAR TODAY!
FIVE THOUSAND?! GEE, I BETTER PLAN A BREAK FOR DINNER! WHERE'S THUH BEST PLACE TO EAT AROUND HERE?
GROWL!
MOE'S IS THE BEST!
HIS PONGAS ARE SOGGY! TRY LOU'S!
JENNY MAKES THE BEST FROPER TOAST!
ONLY IF YOU LIKE STALE BREAD! FOR GOOD FROPER TOAST, GO TO SARAH'S KITCHEN!
I LIKE MOE'S SOGGY PONGAS! WHO ARE YOU TO DISPARAGE THEM?
I'M MOE! THEY ARE NOT SOGGY!

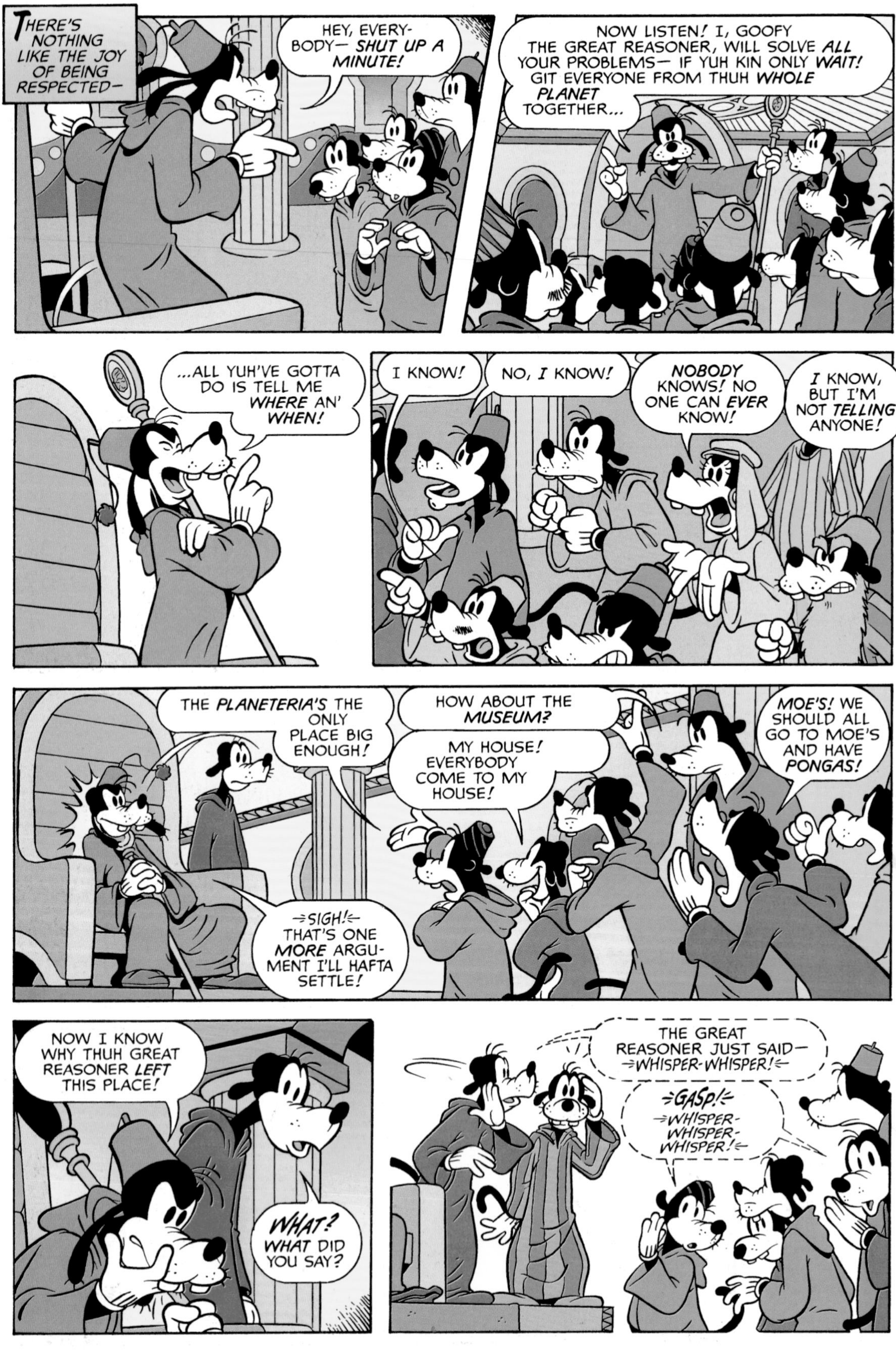
THERE'S NOTHING LIKE THE JOY OF BEING RESPECTED—
HEY, EVERY-BODY— SHUT UP A MINUTE!
NOW LISTEN! I, GOOFY THE GREAT REASONER, WILL SOLVE ALL YOUR PROBLEMS— IF YUH KIN ONLY WAIT! GIT EVERYONE FROM THUH WHOLE PLANET TOGETHER...
...ALL YUH'VE GOTTA DO IS TELL ME WHERE AN' WHEN!
I KNOW!
NO, I KNOW!
NOBODY KNOWS! NO ONE CAN EVER KNOW!
I KNOW, BUT I'M NOT TELLING ANYONE!
THE PLANETERIA'S THE ONLY PLACE BIG ENOUGH!
HOW ABOUT THE MUSEUM?
MY HOUSE! EVERYBODY COME TO MY HOUSE!
MOE'S! WE SHOULD ALL GO TO MOE'S AND HAVE PONGAS!
SIGH! THAT'S ONE MORE ARGU-MENT I'LL HAFTA SETTLE!
NOW I KNOW WHY THUH GREAT REASONER LEFT THIS PLACE!
WHAT? WHAT DID YOU SAY?
THE GREAT REASONER JUST SAID— WHISPER-WHISPER!
GASP! WHISPER-WHISPER-WHISPER!

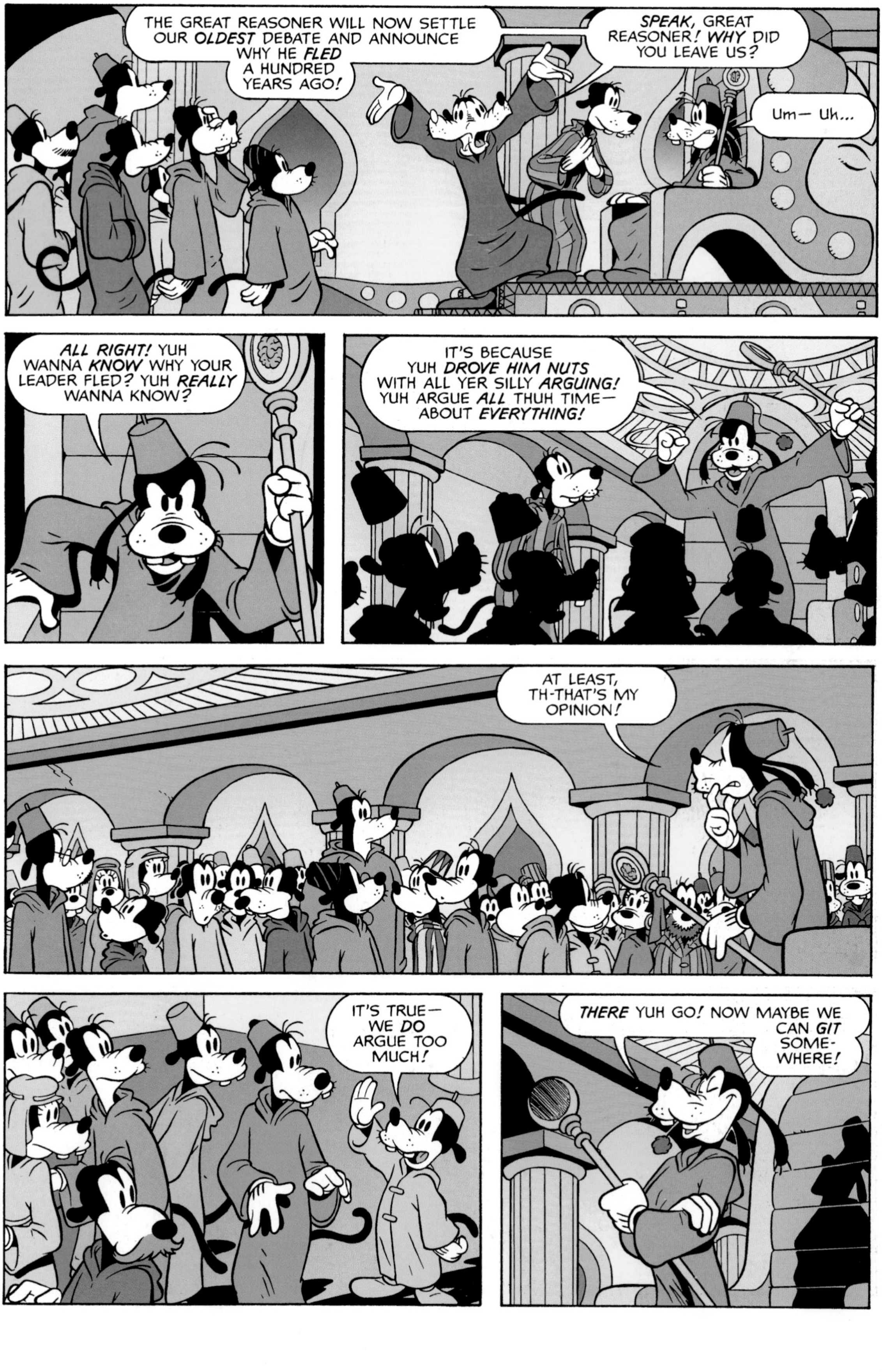
THE GREAT REASONER WILL NOW SETTLE OUR OLDEST DEBATE AND ANNOUNCE WHY HE FLED A HUNDRED YEARS AGO!
SPEAK, GREAT REASONER! WHY DID YOU LEAVE US?
Um— Uh...
ALL RIGHT! YUH WANNA KNOW WHY YOUR LEADER FLED? YUH REALLY WANNA KNOW?
IT'S BECAUSE YUH DROVE HIM NUTS WITH ALL YER SILLY ARGUING! YUH ARGUE ALL THUH TIME— ABOUT EVERYTHING!
AT LEAST, TH-THAT'S MY OPINION!
IT'S TRUE— WE DO ARGUE TOO MUCH!
THERE YUH GO! NOW MAYBE WE CAN GIT SOME-WHERE!

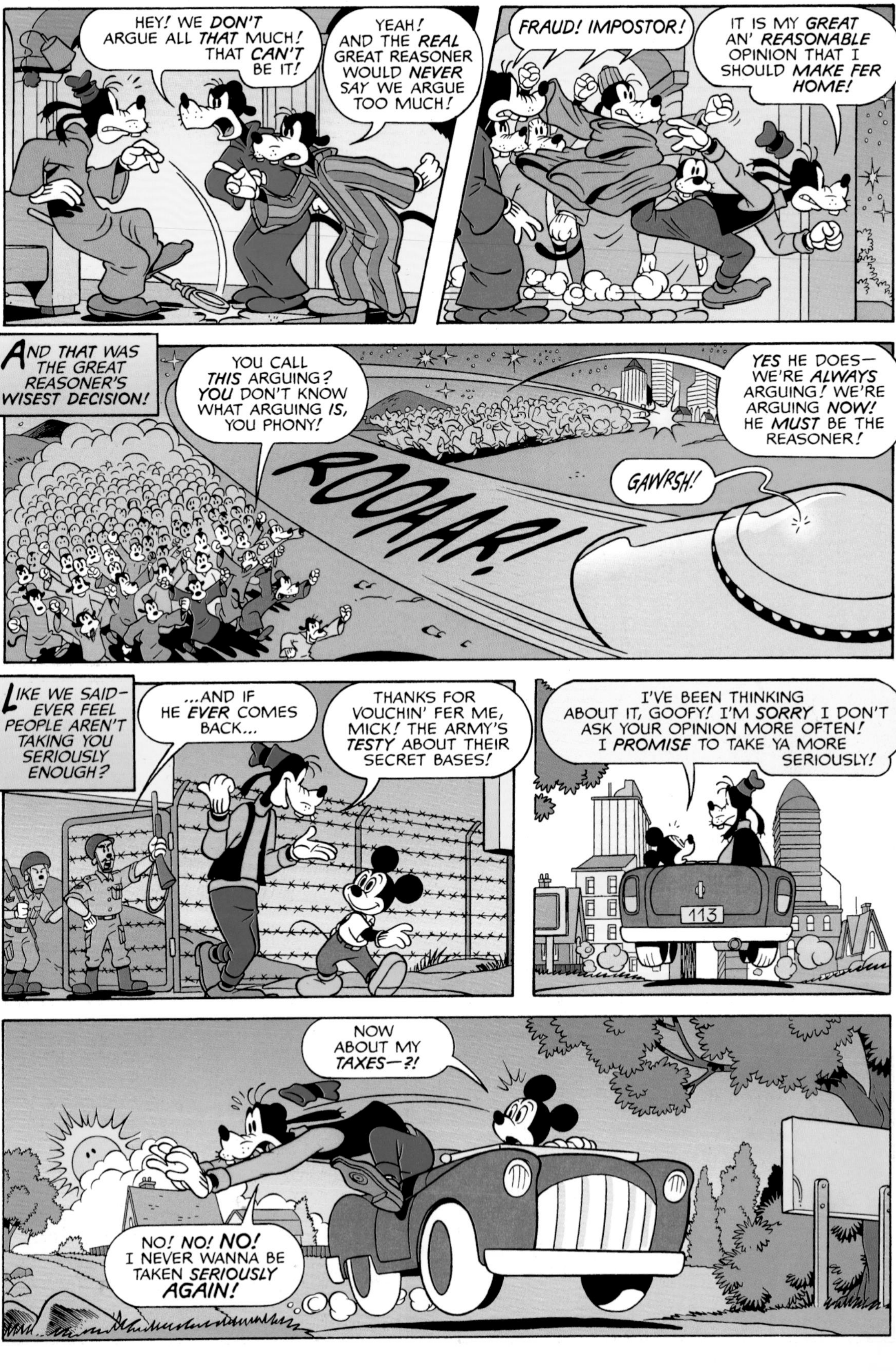
HEY! WE DON'T ARGUE ALL THAT MUCH! THAT CAN'T BE IT!
YEAH! AND THE REAL GREAT REASONER WOULD NEVER SAY WE ARGUE TOO MUCH!
FRAUD! IMPOSTOR!
IT IS MY GREAT AN' REASONABLE OPINION THAT I SHOULD MAKE FER HOME!
AND THAT WAS THE GREAT REASONER'S WISEST DECISION!
YOU CALL THIS ARGUING? YOU DON'T KNOW WHAT ARGUING IS, YOU PHONY!
YES HE DOES— WE'RE ALWAYS ARGUING! WE'RE ARGUING NOW! HE MUST BE THE REASONER!
ROOAAR!
GAWRSH!
LIKE WE SAID- EVER FEEL PEOPLE AREN'T TAKING YOU SERIOUSLY ENOUGH?
...AND IF HE EVER COMES BACK...
THANKS FOR VOUCHIN' FER ME, MICK! THE ARMY'S TESTY ABOUT THEIR SECRET BASES!
I'VE BEEN THINKING ABOUT IT, GOOFY! I'M SORRY I DON'T ASK YOUR OPINION MORE OFTEN! I PROMISE TO TAKE YA MORE SERIOUSLY!
113
NOW ABOUT MY TAXES—?!
NO! NO! NO! I NEVER WANNA BE TAKEN SERIOUSLY AGAIN!

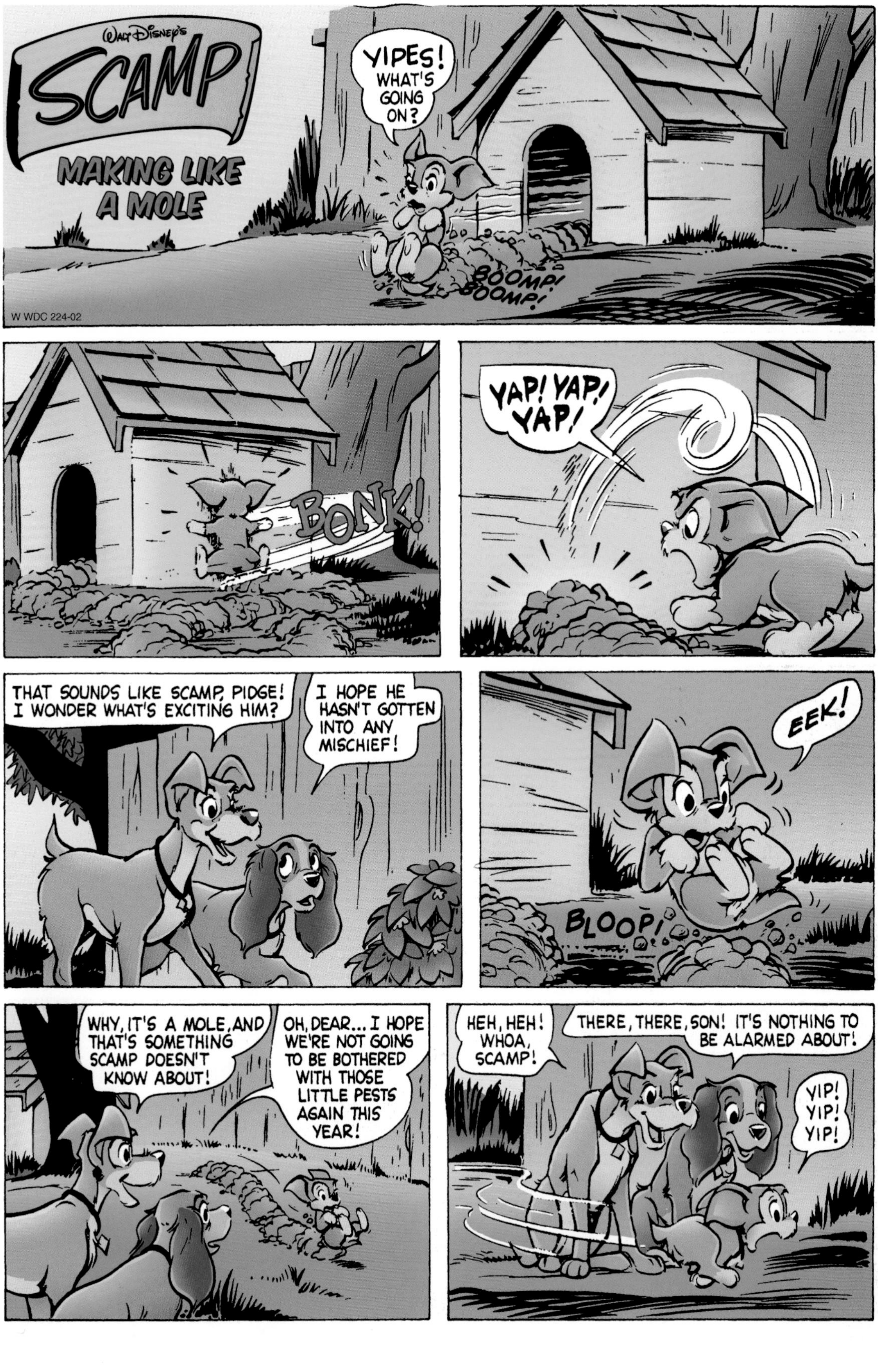
WALT DISNEY'S
SCAMP
MAKING LIKE A MOLE
YIPES! WHAT'S GOING ON?
BOOMP! BOOMP!
W WDC 224-02
BONK!
YAP! YAP! YAP!
THAT SOUNDS LIKE SCAMP, PIDGE! I WONDER WHAT'S EXCITING HIM?
I HOPE HE HASN'T GOTTEN INTO ANY MISCHIEF!
EEK!
BLOOP!
WHY, IT'S A MOLE, AND THAT'S SOMETHING SCAMP DOESN'T KNOW ABOUT!
OH, DEAR... I HOPE WE'RE NOT GOING TO BE BOTHERED WITH THOSE LITTLE PESTS AGAIN THIS YEAR!
HEH, HEH! WHOA, SCAMP!
THERE, THERE, SON! IT'S NOTHING TO BE ALARMED ABOUT!
YIP! YIP! YIP!

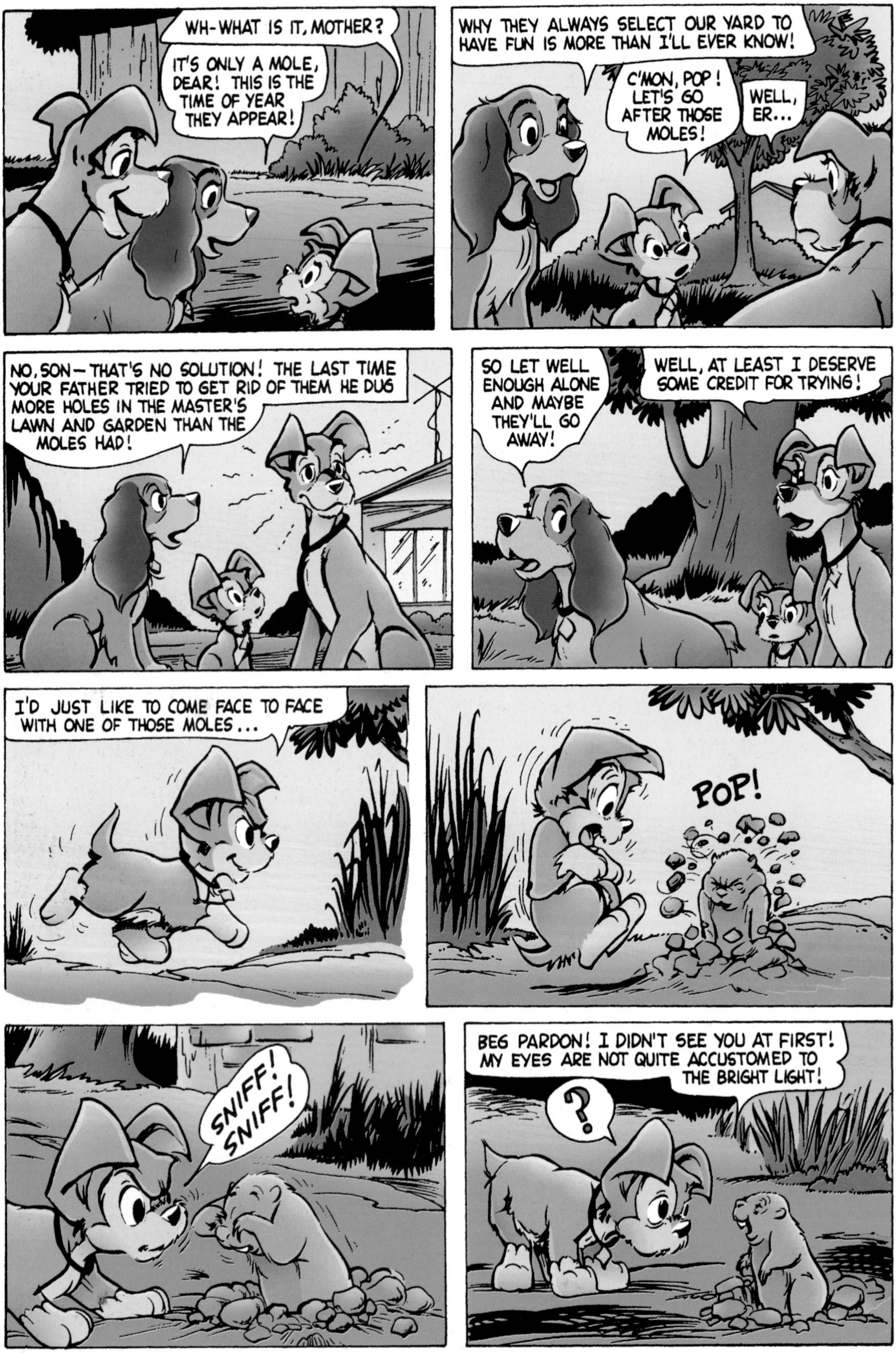
WH-WHAT IS IT, MOTHER?
IT'S ONLY A MOLE, DEAR! THIS IS THE TIME OF YEAR THEY APPEAR!
WHY THEY ALWAYS SELECT OUR YARD TO HAVE FUN IS MORE THAN I'LL EVER KNOW!
C'MON, POP! LET'S GO AFTER THOSE MOLES!
WELL, ER...
NO, SON—THAT'S NO SOLUTION! THE LAST TIME YOUR FATHER TRIED TO GET RID OF THEM HE DUG MORE HOLES IN THE MASTER'S LAWN AND GARDEN THAN THE MOLES HAD!
SO LET WELL ENOUGH ALONE AND MAYBE THEY'LL GO AWAY!
WELL, AT LEAST I DESERVE SOME CREDIT FOR TRYING!
I'D JUST LIKE TO COME FACE TO FACE WITH ONE OF THOSE MOLES...
POP!
SNIFF! SNIFF!
BEG PARDON! I DIDN'T SEE YOU AT FIRST! MY EYES ARE NOT QUITE ACCUSTOMED TO THE BRIGHT LIGHT!
?

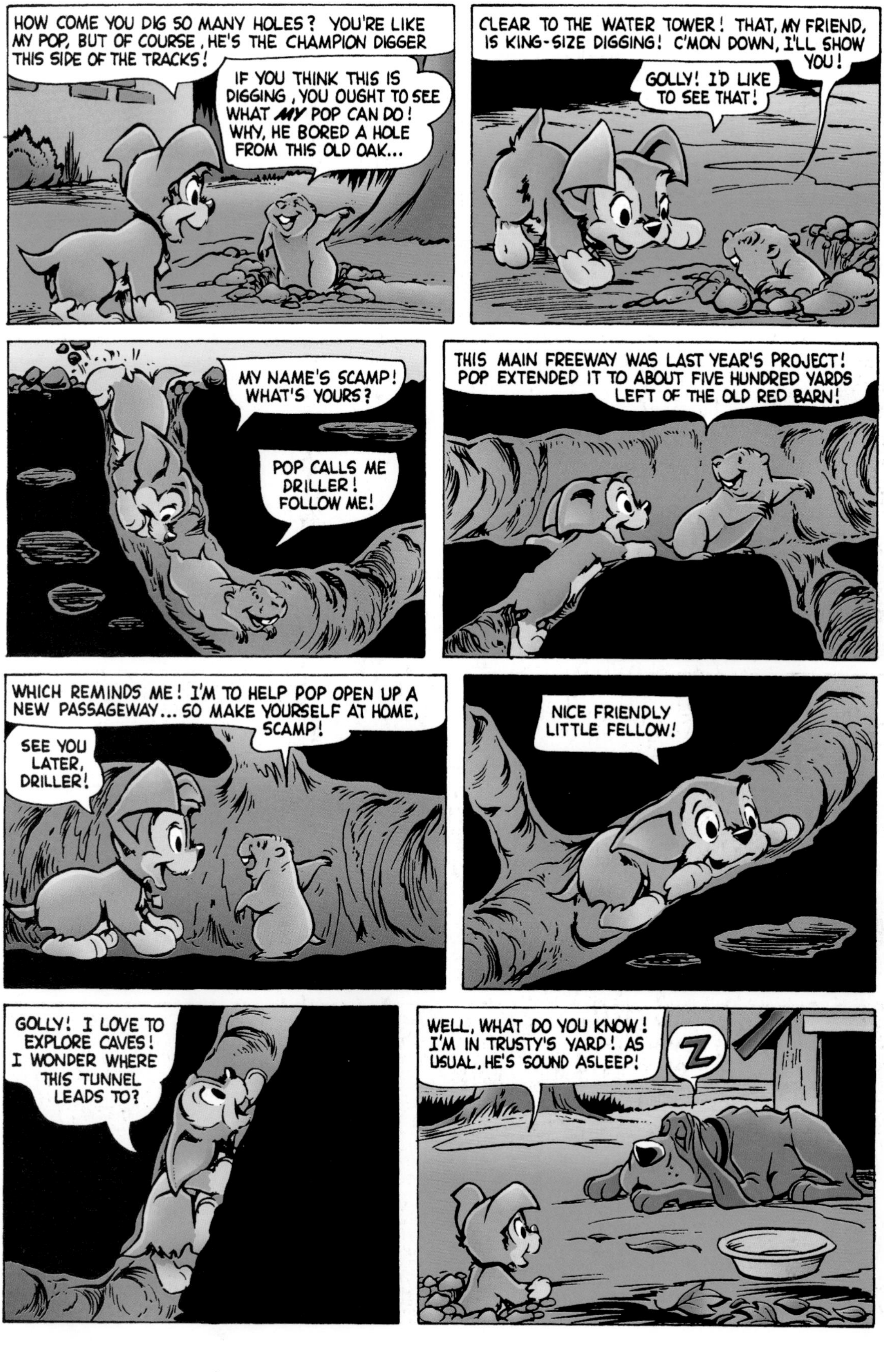
HOW COME YOU DIG SO MANY HOLES? YOU'RE LIKE MY POP, BUT OF COURSE, HE'S THE CHAMPION DIGGER THIS SIDE OF THE TRACKS!
IF YOU THINK THIS IS DIGGING, YOU OUGHT TO SEE WHAT MY POP CAN DO! WHY, HE BORED A HOLE FROM THIS OLD OAK...
CLEAR TO THE WATER TOWER! THAT, MY FRIEND, IS KING-SIZE DIGGING! C'MON DOWN, I'LL SHOW YOU!
GOLLY! I'D LIKE TO SEE THAT!
MY NAME'S SCAMP! WHAT'S YOURS?
POP CALLS ME DRILLER! FOLLOW ME!
THIS MAIN FREEWAY WAS LAST YEAR'S PROJECT! POP EXTENDED IT TO ABOUT FIVE HUNDRED YARDS LEFT OF THE OLD RED BARN!
WHICH REMINDS ME! I'M TO HELP POP OPEN UP A NEW PASSAGEWAY... SO MAKE YOURSELF AT HOME, SCAMP!
SEE YOU LATER, DRILLER!
NICE FRIENDLY LITTLE FELLOW!
GOLLY! I LOVE TO EXPLORE CAVES! I WONDER WHERE THIS TUNNEL LEADS TO?
WELL, WHAT DO YOU KNOW! I'M IN TRUSTY'S YARD! AS USUAL, HE'S SOUND ASLEEP!
Z

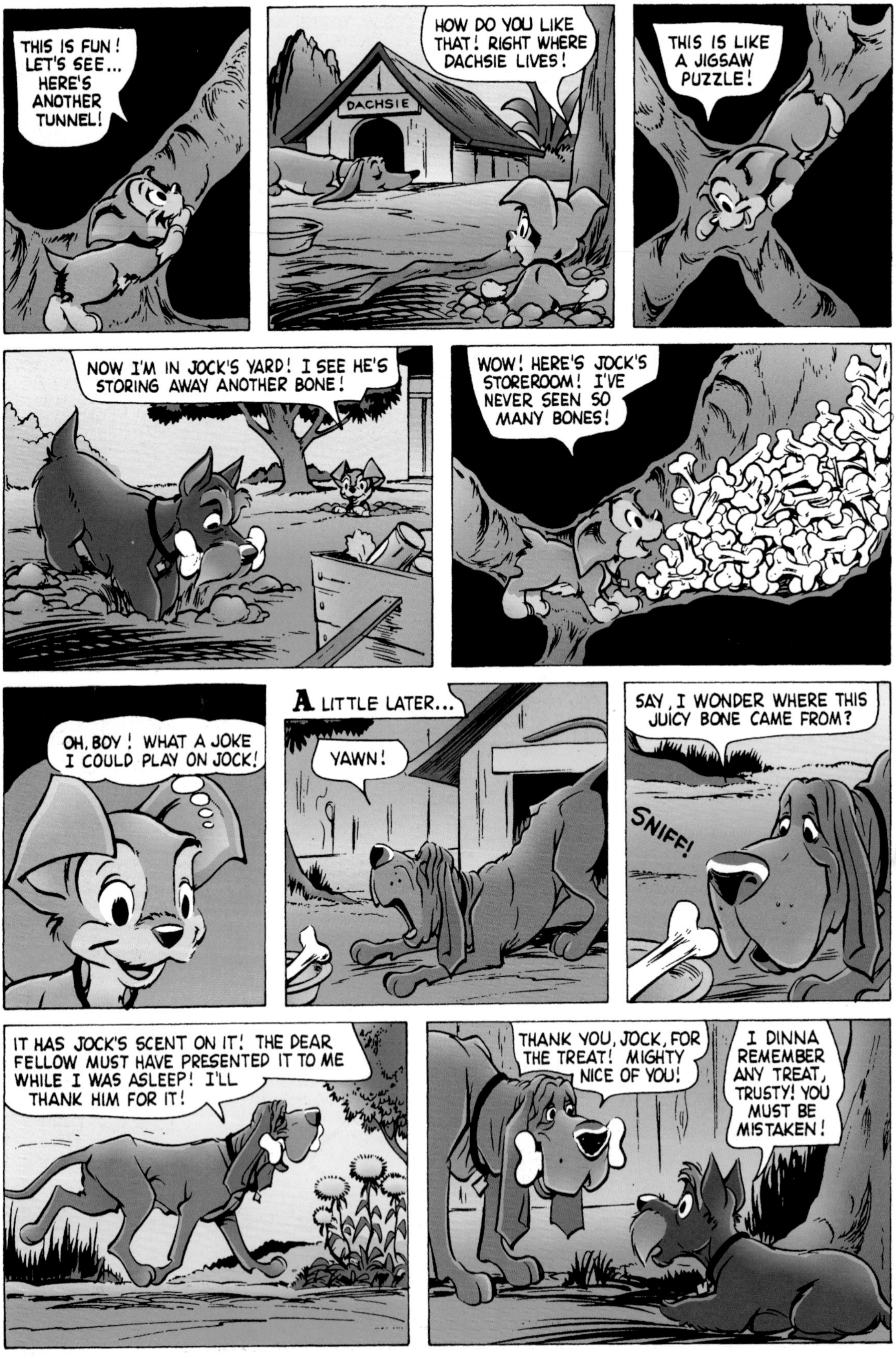
THIS IS FUN! LET'S SEE... HERE'S ANOTHER TUNNEL!
HOW DO YOU LIKE THAT! RIGHT WHERE DACHSIE LIVES!
DACHSIE
THIS IS LIKE A JIGSAW PUZZLE!
NOW I'M IN JOCK'S YARD! I SEE HE'S STORING AWAY ANOTHER BONE!
WOW! HERE'S JOCK'S STOREROOM! I'VE NEVER SEEN SO MANY BONES!
OH, BOY! WHAT A JOKE I COULD PLAY ON JOCK!
A LITTLE LATER...
YAWN!
SAY, I WONDER WHERE THIS JUICY BONE CAME FROM?
SNIFF!
IT HAS JOCK'S SCENT ON IT! THE DEAR FELLOW MUST HAVE PRESENTED IT TO ME WHILE I WAS ASLEEP! I'LL THANK HIM FOR IT!
THANK YOU, JOCK, FOR THE TREAT! MIGHTY NICE OF YOU!
I DINNA REMEMBER ANY TREAT, TRUSTY! YOU MUST BE MISTAKEN!

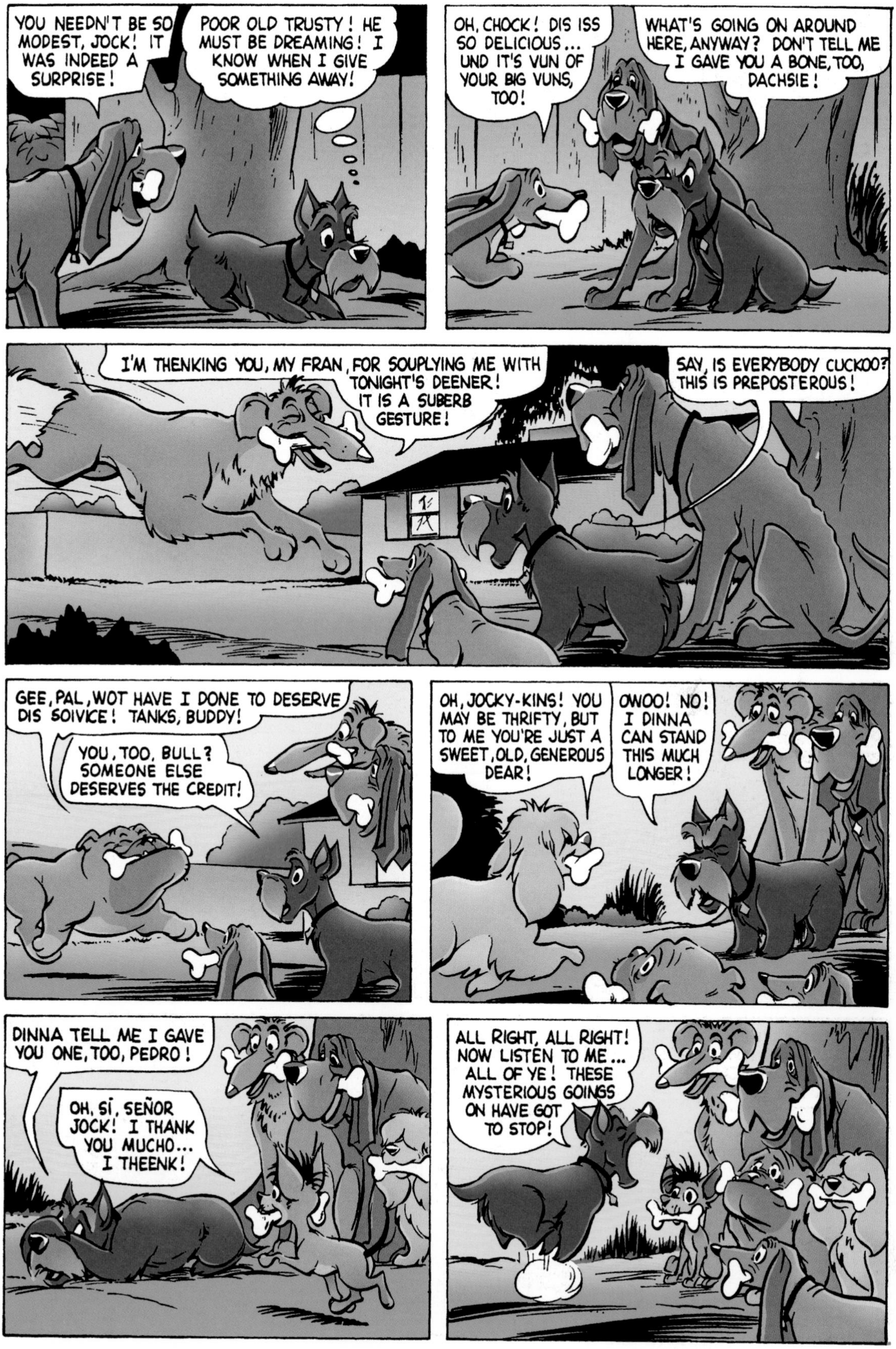
YOU NEEDN'T BE SO MODEST, JOCK! IT WAS INDEED A SURPRISE!
POOR OLD TRUSTY! HE MUST BE DREAMING! I KNOW WHEN I GIVE SOMETHING AWAY!
OH, CHOCK! DIS ISS SO DELICIOUS... UND IT'S VUN OF YOUR BIG VUNS, TOO!
WHAT'S GOING ON AROUND HERE, ANYWAY? DON'T TELL ME I GAVE YOU A BONE, TOO, DACHSIE!
I'M THENKING YOU, MY FRAN, FOR SOUPLYING ME WITH TONIGHT'S DEENER! IT IS A SUBERB GESTURE!
SAY, IS EVERYBODY CUCKOO? THIS IS PREPOSTEROUS!
GEE, PAL, WOT HAVE I DONE TO DESERVE DIS SOIVICE! TANKS, BUDDY!
YOU, TOO, BULL? SOMEONE ELSE DESERVES THE CREDIT!
OH, JOCKY-KINS! YOU MAY BE THRIFTY, BUT TO ME YOU'RE JUST A SWEET, OLD, GENEROUS DEAR!
OWOO! NO! I DINNA CAN STAND THIS MUCH LONGER!
DINNA TELL ME I GAVE YOU ONE, TOO, PEDRO!
OH, SÍ, SEÑOR JOCK! I THANK YOU MUCHO... I THEENK!
ALL RIGHT, ALL RIGHT! NOW LISTEN TO ME... ALL OF YE! THESE MYSTERIOUS GOINGS ON HAVE GOT TO STOP!

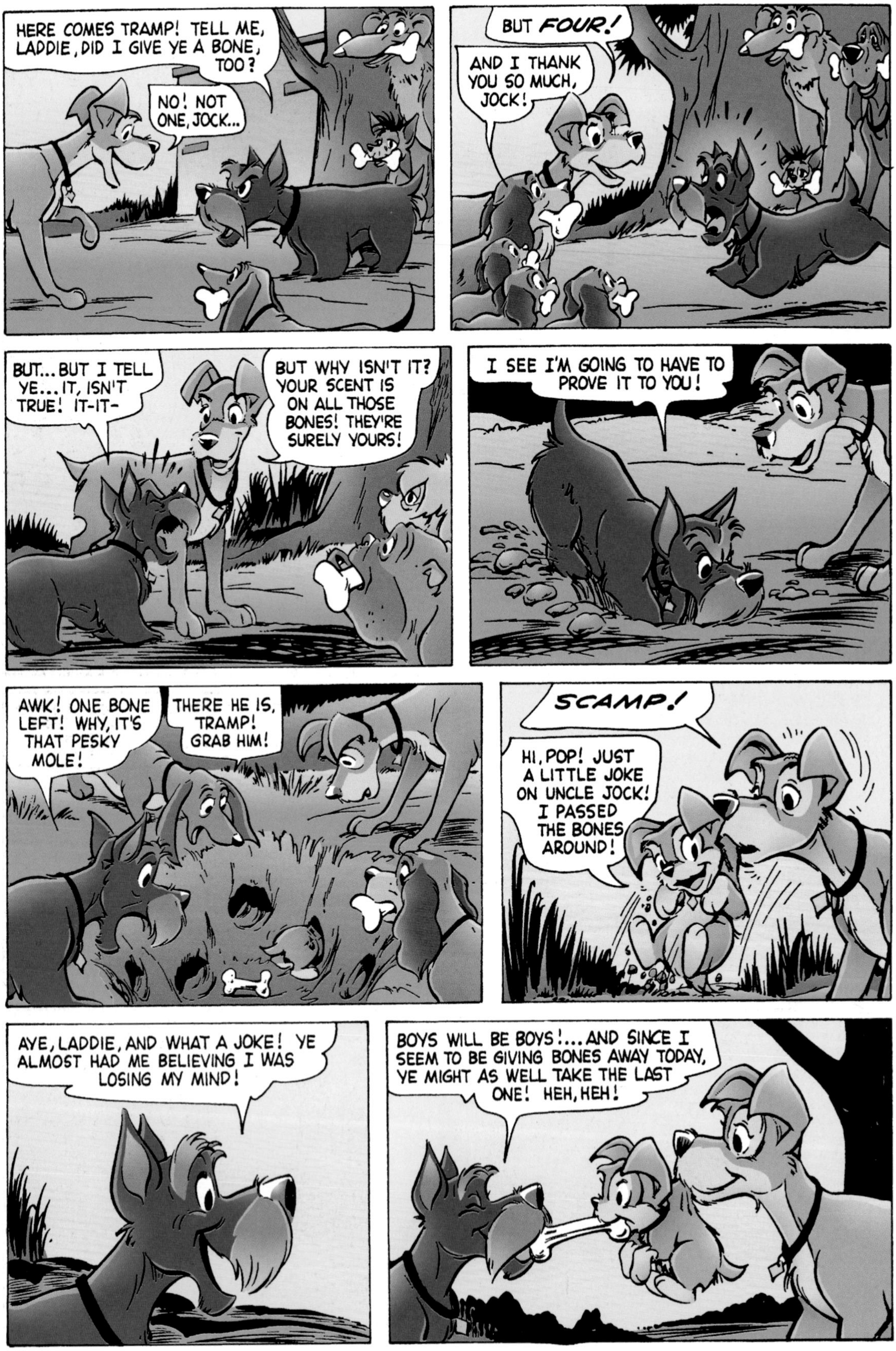

HERE COMES TRAMP! TELL ME, LADDIE, DID I GIVE YE A BONE, TOO?
NO! NOT ONE, JOCK...
BUT FOUR!
AND I THANK YOU SO MUCH, JOCK!
BUT... BUT I TELL YE... IT, ISN'T TRUE! IT-IT-
BUT WHY ISN'T IT? YOUR SCENT IS ON ALL THOSE BONES! THEY'RE SURELY YOURS!
I SEE I'M GOING TO HAVE TO PROVE IT TO YOU!
AWK! ONE BONE LEFT! WHY, IT'S THAT PESKY MOLE!
THERE HE IS, TRAMP! GRAB HIM!
SCAMP!
HI, POP! JUST A LITTLE JOKE ON UNCLE JOCK! I PASSED THE BONES AROUND!
AYE, LADDIE, AND WHAT A JOKE! YE ALMOST HAD ME BELIEVING I WAS LOSING MY MIND!
BOYS WILL BE BOYS!... AND SINCE I SEEM TO BE GIVING BONES AWAY TODAY, YE MIGHT AS WELL TAKE THE LAST ONE! HEH, HEH!

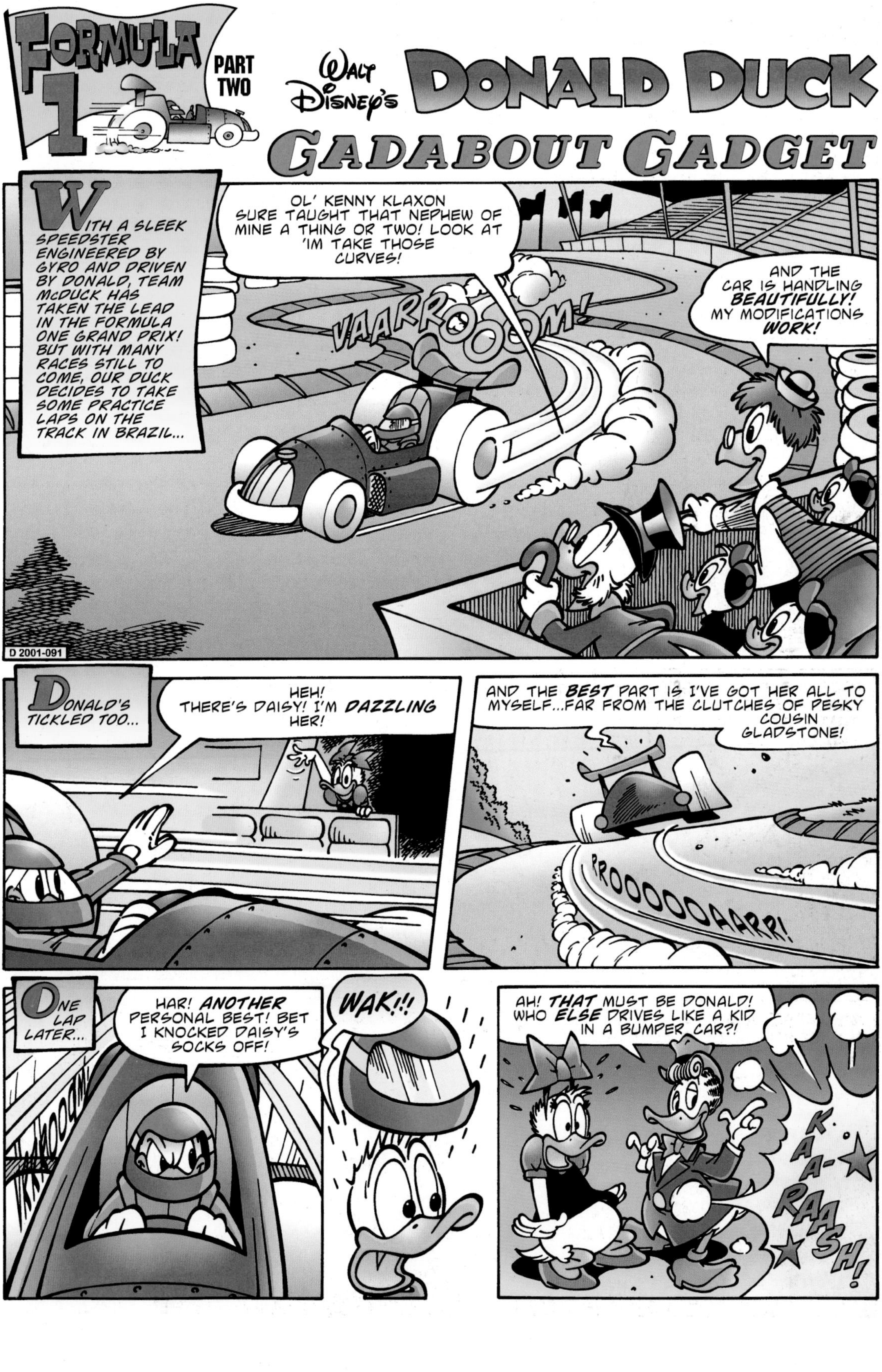
FORMULA 1
PART TWO
Walt Disney's DONALD DUCK
GADABOUT GADGET
WITH A SLEEK SPEEDSTER ENGINEERED BY GYRO AND DRIVEN BY DONALD, TEAM McDUCK HAS TAKEN THE LEAD IN THE FORMULA ONE GRAND PRIX! BUT WITH MANY RACES STILL TO COME, OUR DUCK DECIDES TO TAKE SOME PRACTICE LAPS ON THE TRACK IN BRAZIL...
OL' KENNY KLAXON SURE TAUGHT THAT NEPHEW OF MINE A THING OR TWO! LOOK AT 'IM TAKE THOSE CURVES!
VAARROOOOM!
AND THE CAR IS HANDLING BEAUTIFULLY! MY MODIFICATIONS WORK!
D 2001-091
DONALD'S TICKLED TOO...
HEH! THERE'S DAISY! I'M DAZZLING HER!
AND THE BEST PART IS I'VE GOT HER ALL TO MYSELF...FAR FROM THE CLUTCHES OF PESKY COUSIN GLADSTONE!
RROOOOOOAARR!
ONE LAP LATER...
HAR! ANOTHER PERSONAL BEST! BET I KNOCKED DAISY'S SOCKS OFF!
WAK!!!
AH! THAT MUST BE DONALD! WHO ELSE DRIVES LIKE A KID IN A BUMPER CAR?!
KAA-RAASH!

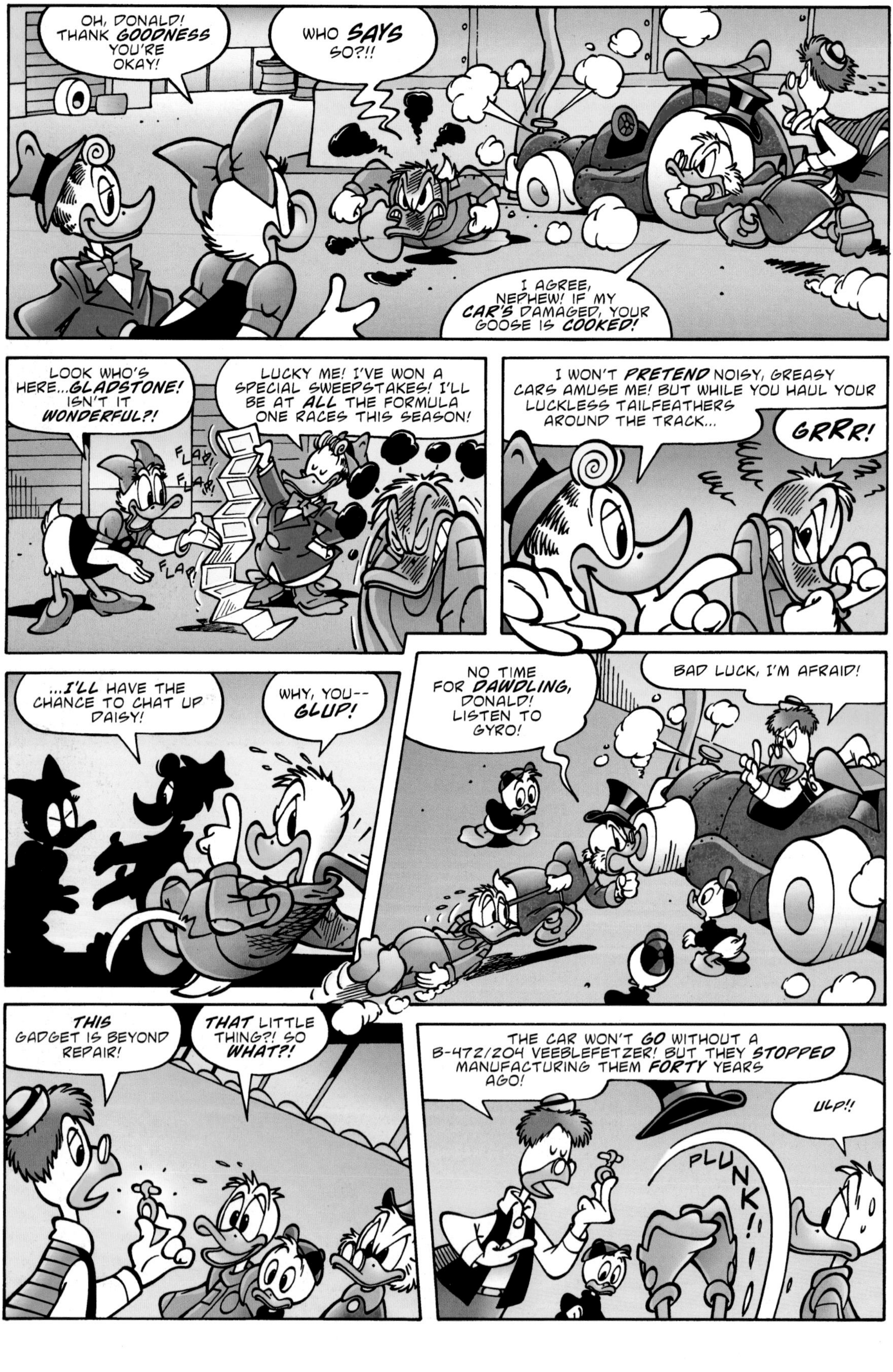

OH, DONALD! THANK GOODNESS YOU'RE OKAY!
WHO SAYS SO?!!
I AGREE, NEPHEW! IF MY CAR'S DAMAGED, YOUR GOOSE IS COOKED!
LOOK WHO'S HERE...GLADSTONE! ISN'T IT WONDERFUL?!
LUCKY ME! I'VE WON A SPECIAL SWEEPSTAKES! I'LL BE AT ALL THE FORMULA ONE RACES THIS SEASON!
FLAP! FLAP! FLAP!
I WON'T PRETEND NOISY, GREASY CARS AMUSE ME! BUT WHILE YOU HAUL YOUR LUCKLESS TAILFEATHERS AROUND THE TRACK...
GRRR!
...I'LL HAVE THE CHANCE TO CHAT UP DAISY!
WHY, YOU-- GLUP!
NO TIME FOR DAWDLING, DONALD! LISTEN TO GYRO!
BAD LUCK, I'M AFRAID!
THIS GADGET IS BEYOND REPAIR!
THAT LITTLE THING?! SO WHAT?!
THE CAR WON'T GO WITHOUT A B-472/204 VEEBLEFETZER! BUT THEY STOPPED MANUFACTURING THEM FORTY YEARS AGO!
ULP!!
PLUNK!!

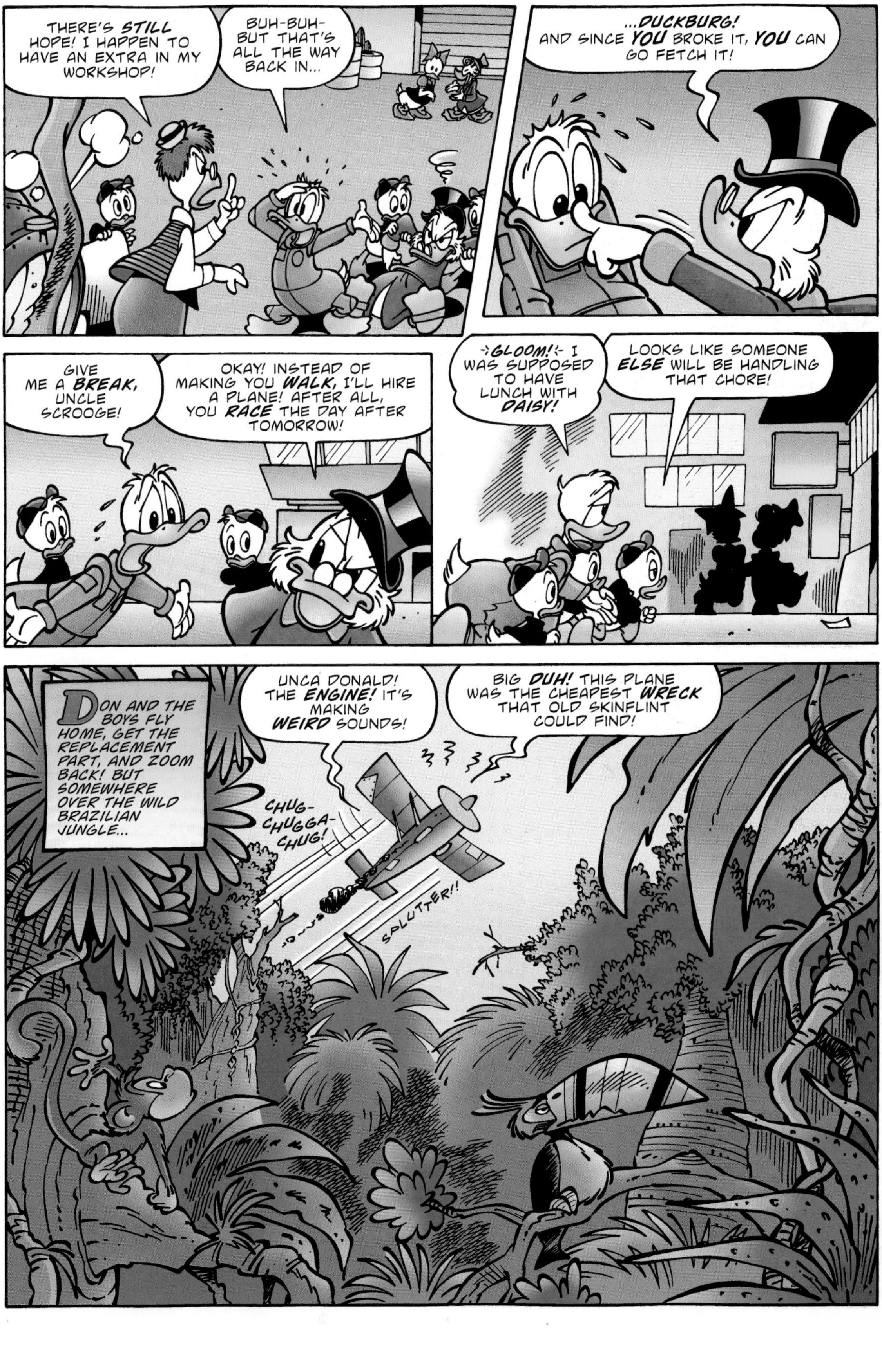
THERE'S STILL HOPE! I HAPPEN TO HAVE AN EXTRA IN MY WORKSHOP!
BUH-BUH-BUT THAT'S ALL THE WAY BACK IN...
...DUCKBURG! AND SINCE YOU BROKE IT, YOU CAN GO FETCH IT!
GIVE ME A BREAK, UNCLE SCROOGE!
OKAY! INSTEAD OF MAKING YOU WALK, I'LL HIRE A PLANE! AFTER ALL, YOU RACE THE DAY AFTER TOMORROW!
-GLOOM!- I WAS SUPPOSED TO HAVE LUNCH WITH DAISY!
LOOKS LIKE SOMEONE ELSE WILL BE HANDLING THAT CHORE!
DON AND THE BOYS FLY HOME, GET THE REPLACEMENT PART, AND ZOOM BACK! BUT SOMEWHERE OVER THE WILD BRAZILIAN JUNGLE...
UNCA DONALD! THE ENGINE! IT'S MAKING WEIRD SOUNDS!
BIG DUH! THIS PLANE WAS THE CHEAPEST WRECK THAT OLD SKINFLINT COULD FIND!
CHUG-CHUGGA-CHUG!
SPLUTTER!!

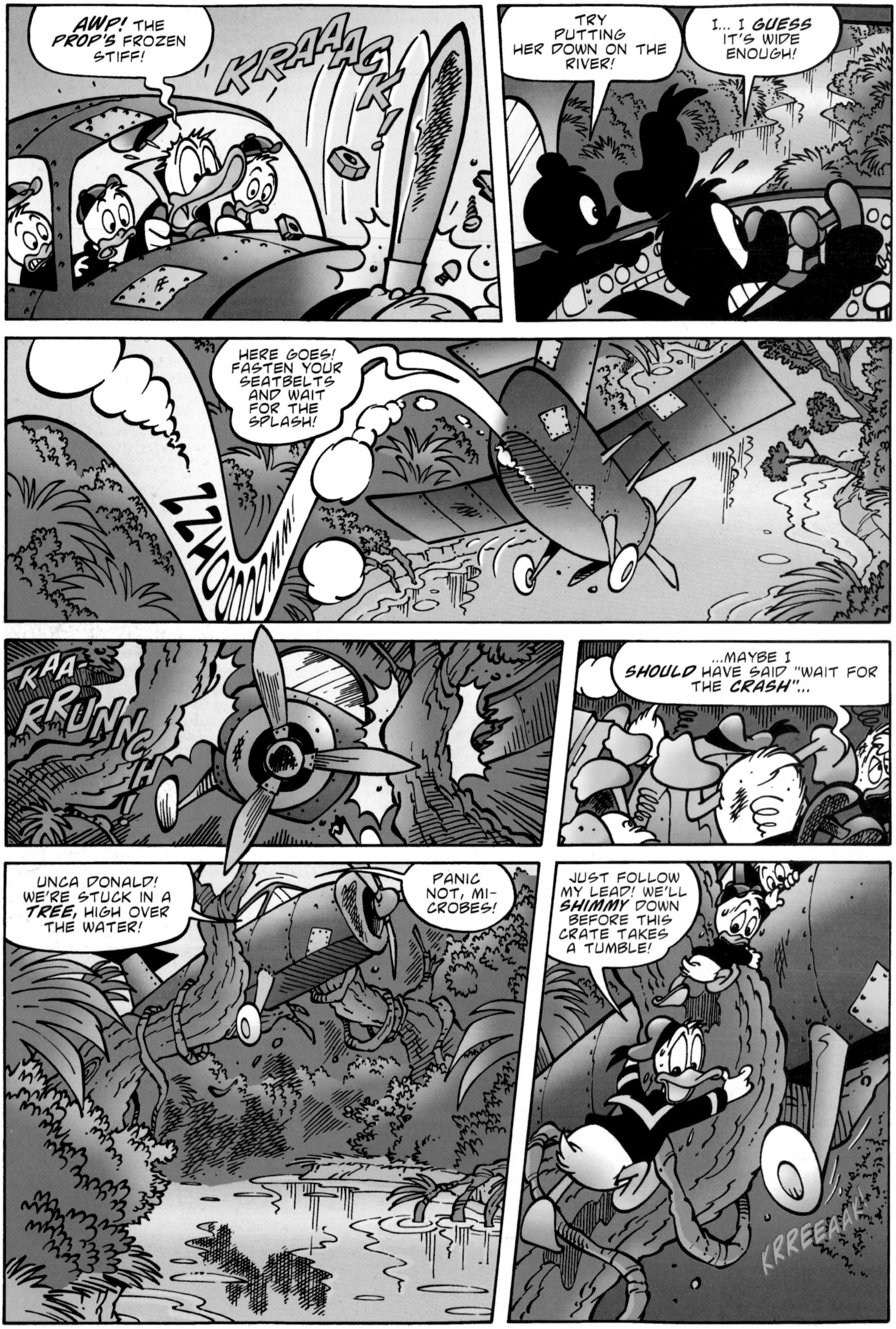
AWP! THE PROP'S FROZEN STIFF!
KRAAAACK!
TRY PUTTING HER DOWN ON THE RIVER!
I... I GUESS IT'S WIDE ENOUGH!
HERE GOES! FASTEN YOUR SEATBELTS AND WAIT FOR THE SPLASH!
ZZHOOOOOMM!
KAA-RRUNNCH!
...MAYBE I SHOULD HAVE SAID "WAIT FOR THE CRASH"...
UNCA DONALD! WE'RE STUCK IN A TREE, HIGH OVER THE WATER!
PANIC NOT, MI-CROBES!
JUST FOLLOW MY LEAD! WE'LL SHIMMY DOWN BEFORE THIS CRATE TAKES A TUMBLE!
KRREEAAK

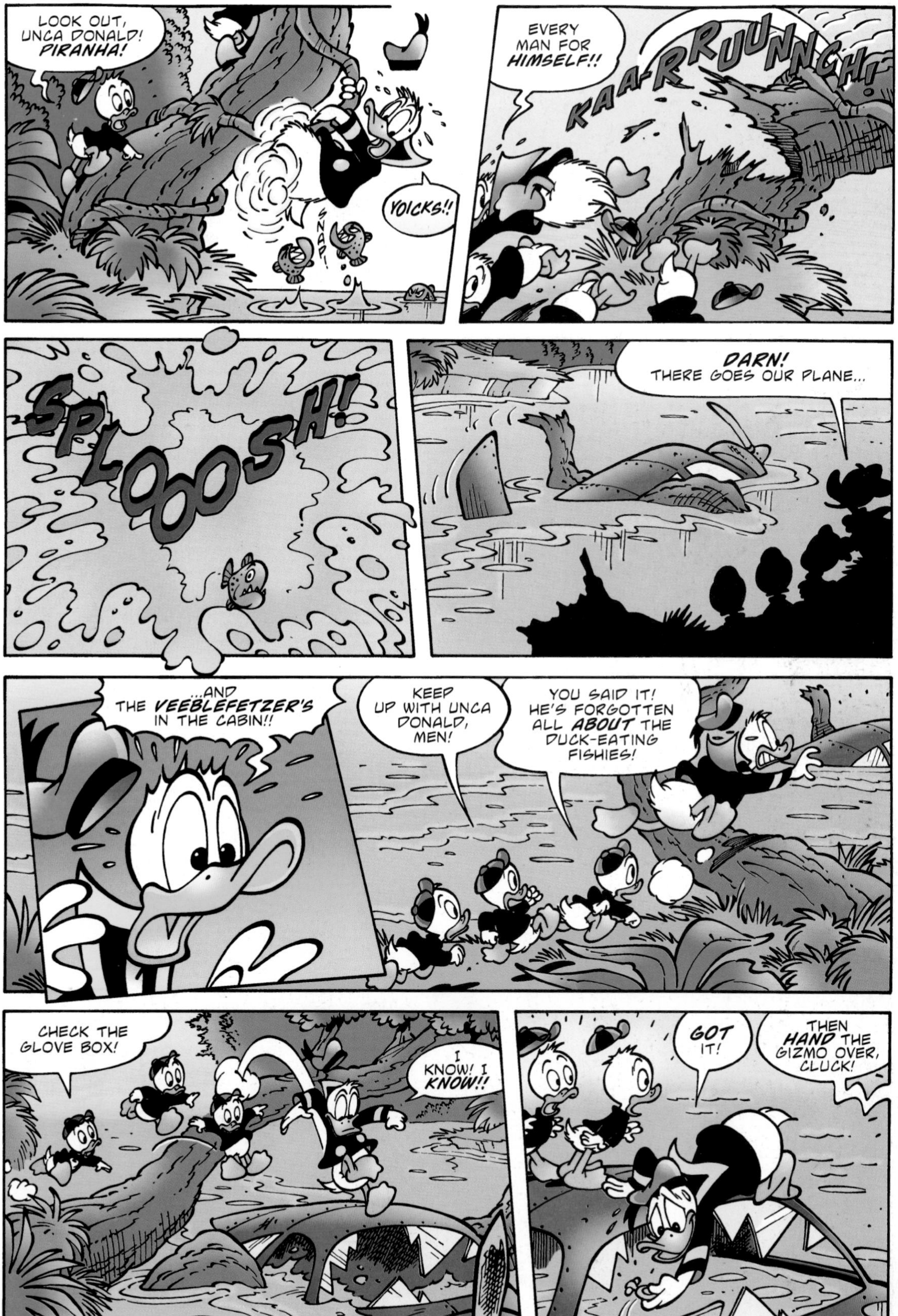

LOOK OUT, UNCA DONALD! PIRANHA!
SNAP!
YOICKS!!
EVERY MAN FOR HIMSELF!!
KAA-RRUUNNCH!
SPLOOOSH!
DARN! THERE GOES OUR PLANE...
...AND THE VEEBLEFETZER'S IN THE CABIN!!
KEEP UP WITH UNCA DONALD, MEN!
YOU SAID IT! HE'S FORGOTTEN ALL ABOUT THE DUCK-EATING FISHIES!
CHECK THE GLOVE BOX!
I KNOW! I KNOW!!
GOT IT!
THEN HAND THE GIZMO OVER, CLUCK!

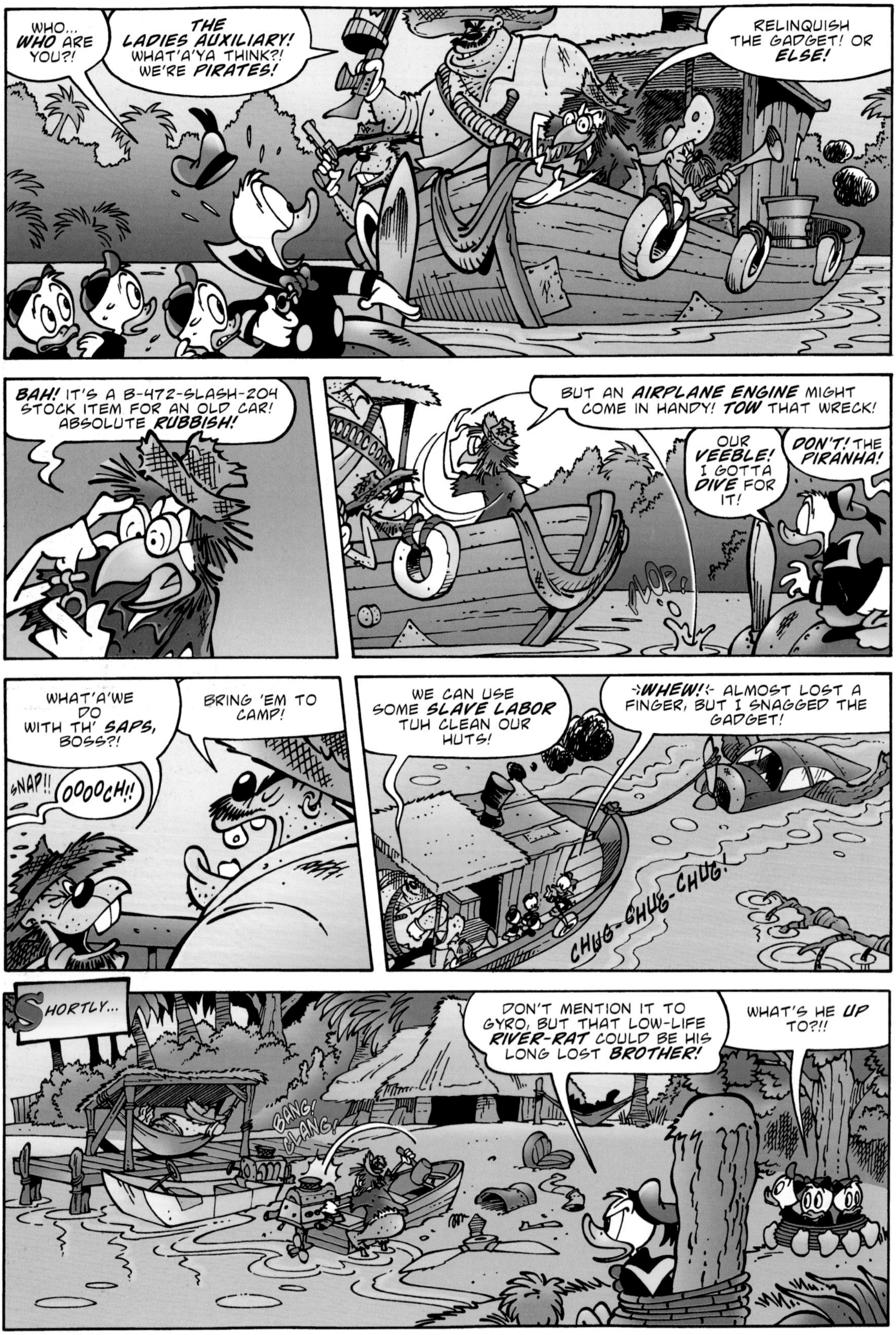
WHO... WHO ARE YOU?!
THE LADIES AUXILIARY! WHAT'A'YA THINK?! WE'RE PIRATES!
RELINQUISH THE GADGET! OR ELSE!
BAH! IT'S A B-472-SLASH-204 STOCK ITEM FOR AN OLD CAR! ABSOLUTE RUBBISH!
BUT AN AIRPLANE ENGINE MIGHT COME IN HANDY! TOW THAT WRECK!
OUR VEEBLE! I GOTTA DIVE FOR IT!
DON'T! THE PIRANHA!
PLOP!
WHAT'A'WE DO WITH TH' SAPS, BOSS?!
BRING 'EM TO CAMP!
SNAP!!
OOOOCH!!
WE CAN USE SOME SLAVE LABOR TUH CLEAN OUR HUTS!
WHEW! ALMOST LOST A FINGER, BUT I SNAGGED THE GADGET!
CHUG-CHUG-CHUG!
SHORTLY...
DON'T MENTION IT TO GYRO, BUT THAT LOW-LIFE RIVER-RAT COULD BE HIS LONG LOST BROTHER!
WHAT'S HE UP TO?!!
BANG! CLANG!

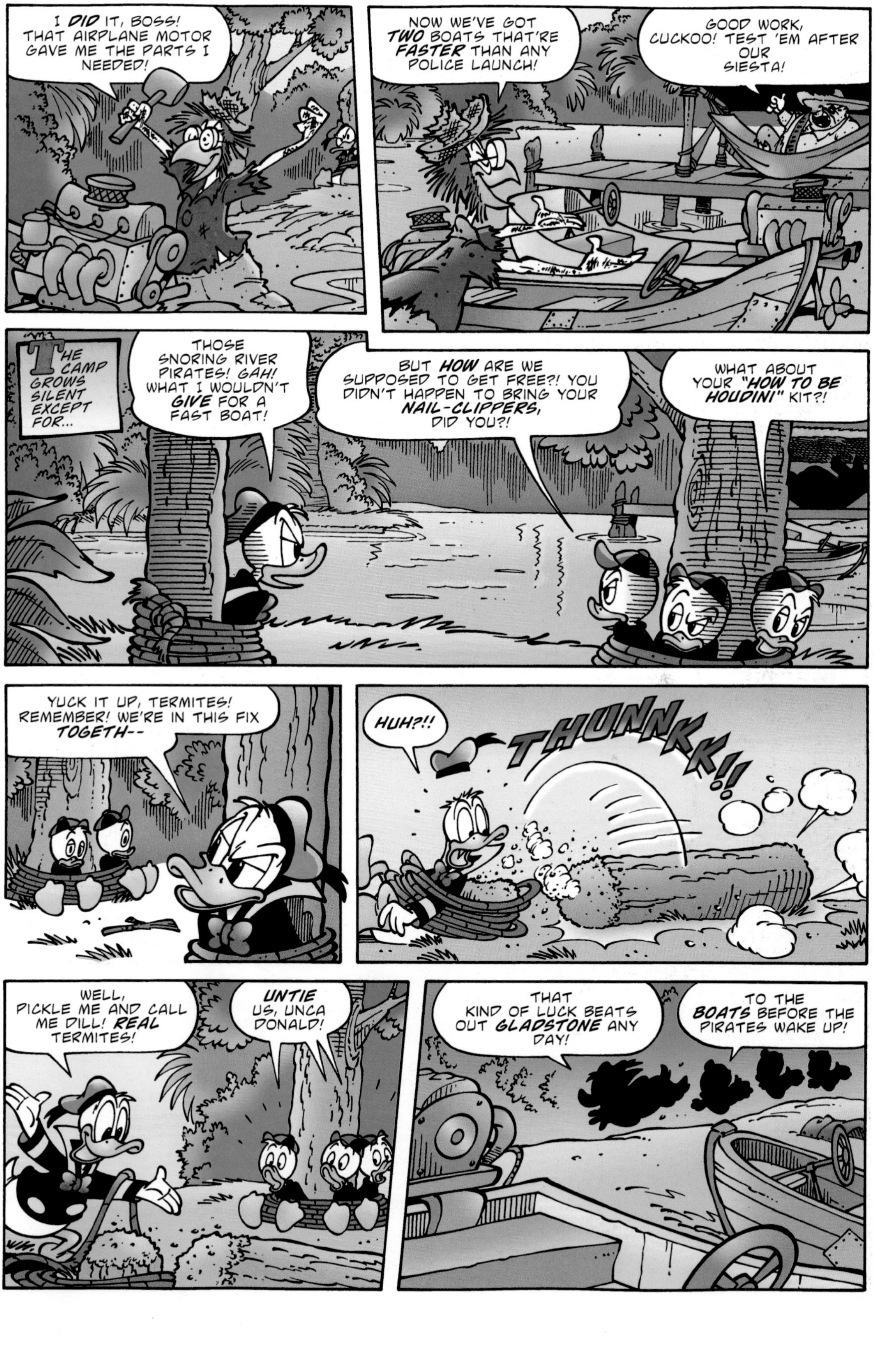

I DID IT, BOSS! THAT AIRPLANE MOTOR GAVE ME THE PARTS I NEEDED!
NOW WE'VE GOT TWO BOATS THAT'RE FASTER THAN ANY POLICE LAUNCH!
GOOD WORK, CUCKOO! TEST 'EM AFTER OUR SIESTA!
THE CAMP GROWS SILENT EXCEPT FOR...
THOSE SNORING RIVER PIRATES! GAH! WHAT I WOULDN'T GIVE FOR A FAST BOAT!
BUT HOW ARE WE SUPPOSED TO GET FREE?! YOU DIDN'T HAPPEN TO BRING YOUR NAIL-CLIPPERS, DID YOU?!
WHAT ABOUT YOUR "HOW TO BE HOUDINI" KIT?!
YUCK IT UP, TERMITES! REMEMBER! WE'RE IN THIS FIX TOGETH--
HUH?!!
THUNNKK!!
WELL, PICKLE ME AND CALL ME DILL! REAL TERMITES!
UNTIE US, UNCA DONALD!
THAT KIND OF LUCK BEATS OUT GLADSTONE ANY DAY!
TO THE BOATS BEFORE THE PIRATES WAKE UP!

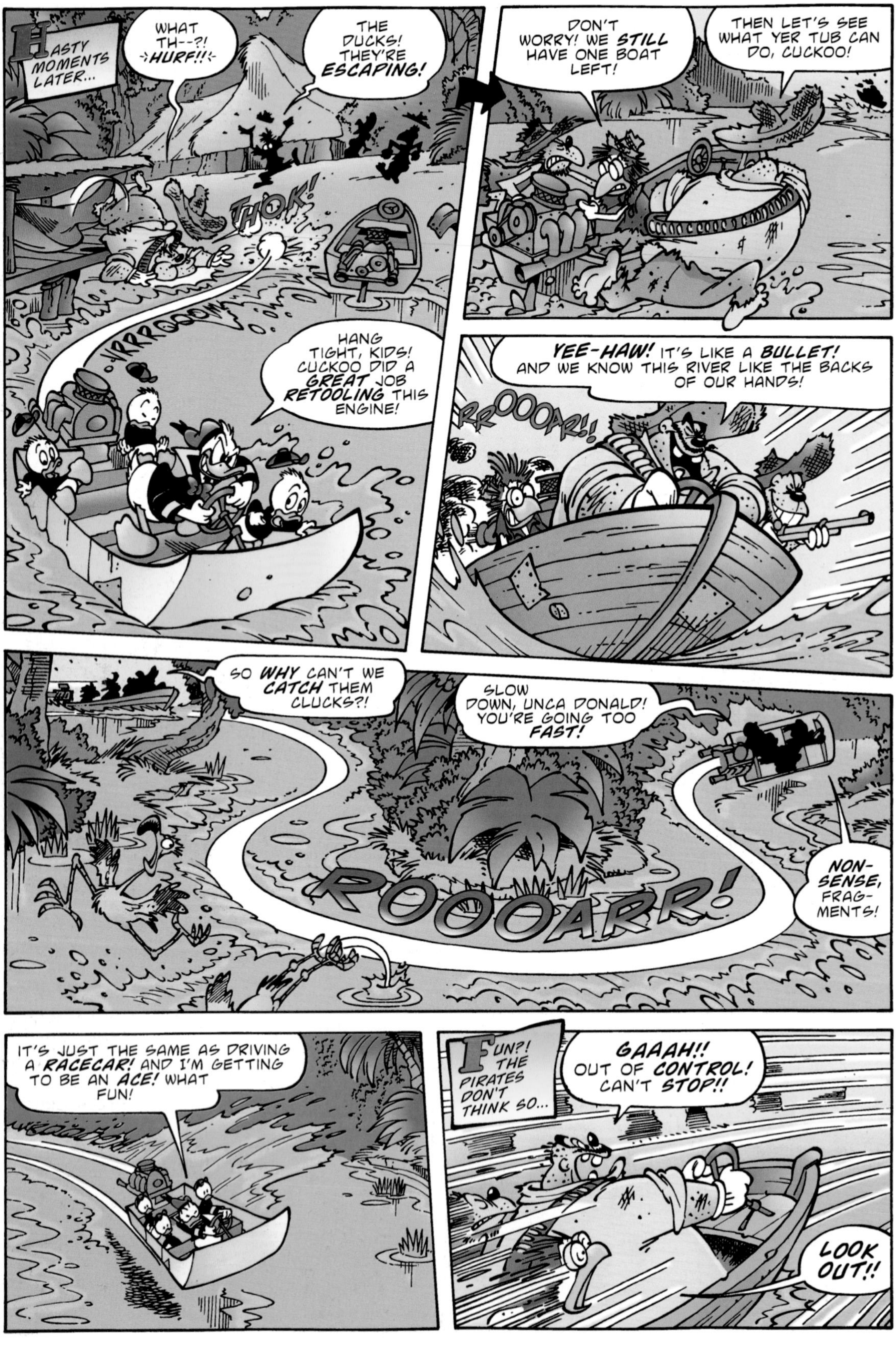
HASTY MOMENTS LATER...
WHAT TH--?! HURF!!
THE DUCKS! THEY'RE ESCAPING!
THOK!
VRRROOOM
HANG TIGHT, KIDS! CUCKOO DID A GREAT JOB RETOOLING THIS ENGINE!
DON'T WORRY! WE STILL HAVE ONE BOAT LEFT!
THEN LET'S SEE WHAT YER TUB CAN DO, CUCKOO!
YEE-HAW! IT'S LIKE A BULLET! AND WE KNOW THIS RIVER LIKE THE BACKS OF OUR HANDS!
RROOOOAR!!
SO WHY CAN'T WE CATCH THEM CLUCKS?!
SLOW DOWN, UNCA DONALD! YOU'RE GOING TOO FAST!
NON-SENSE, FRAG-MENTS!
ROOOARR!
IT'S JUST THE SAME AS DRIVING A RACECAR! AND I'M GETTING TO BE AN ACE! WHAT FUN!
FUN?! THE PIRATES DON'T THINK SO...
GAAAH!! OUT OF CONTROL! CAN'T STOP!!
LOOK OUT!!

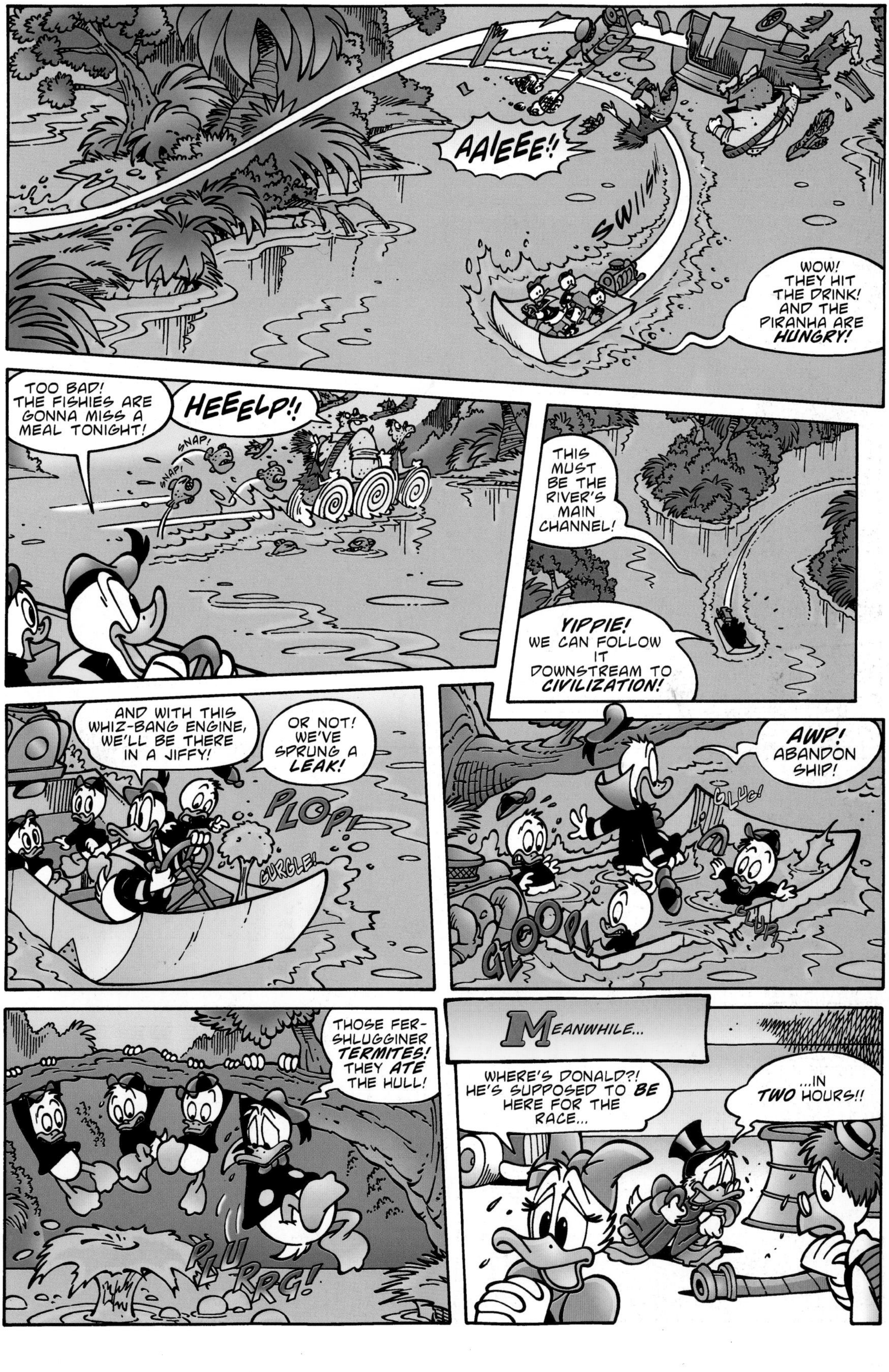

AAIEEE!!
SWISH
WOW! THEY HIT THE DRINK! AND THE PIRANHA ARE HUNGRY!
TOO BAD! THE FISHIES ARE GONNA MISS A MEAL TONIGHT!
HEEELP!!
SNAP!
SNAP!
THIS MUST BE THE RIVER'S MAIN CHANNEL!
YIPPIE! WE CAN FOLLOW IT DOWNSTREAM TO CIVILIZATION!
AND WITH THIS WHIZ-BANG ENGINE, WE'LL BE THERE IN A JIFFY!
OR NOT! WE'VE SPRUNG A LEAK!
PLOP!
GURGLE!
AWP! ABANDON SHIP!
GLUG!
GLOOP!
GLUB
THOSE FER-SHLUGGINER TERMITES! THEY ATE THE HULL!
PLURRG!
MEANWHILE...
WHERE'S DONALD?! HE'S SUPPOSED TO BE HERE FOR THE RACE...
...IN TWO HOURS!!

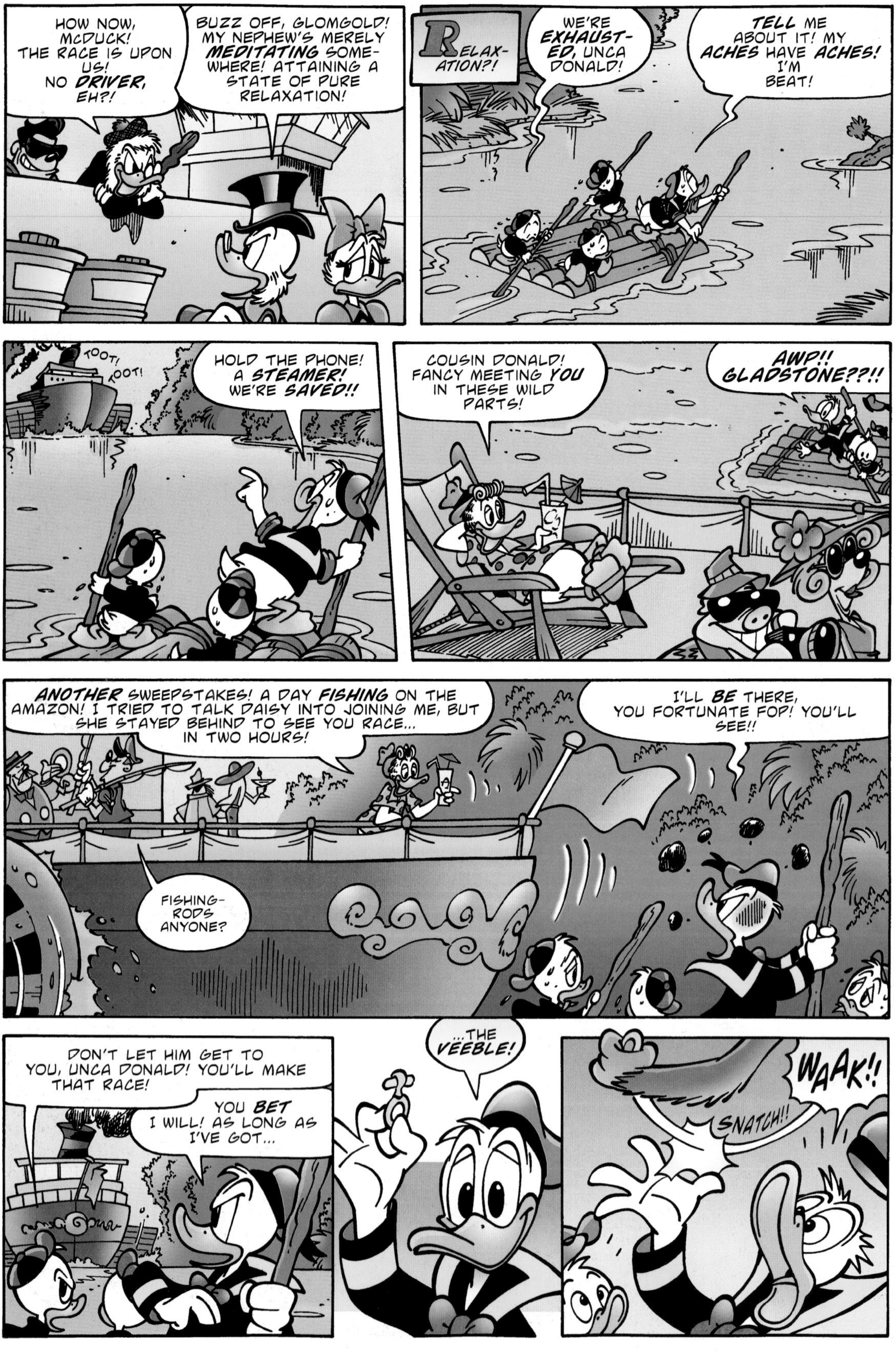
HOW NOW, McDUCK! THE RACE IS UPON US! NO DRIVER, EH?!
BUZZ OFF, GLOMGOLD! MY NEPHEW'S MERELY MEDITATING SOMEWHERE! ATTAINING A STATE OF PURE RELAXATION!
RELAXATION?!
WE'RE EXHAUSTED, UNCA DONALD!
TELL ME ABOUT IT! MY ACHES HAVE ACHES! I'M BEAT!
TOOT! TOOT!
HOLD THE PHONE! A STEAMER! WE'RE SAVED!!
COUSIN DONALD! FANCY MEETING YOU IN THESE WILD PARTS!
AWP!! GLADSTONE??!!
ANOTHER SWEEPSTAKES! A DAY FISHING ON THE AMAZON! I TRIED TO TALK DAISY INTO JOINING ME, BUT SHE STAYED BEHIND TO SEE YOU RACE... IN TWO HOURS!
I'LL BE THERE, YOU FORTUNATE FOP! YOU'LL SEE!!
FISHING-RODS ANYONE?
DON'T LET HIM GET TO YOU, UNCA DONALD! YOU'LL MAKE THAT RACE!
YOU BET I WILL! AS LONG AS I'VE GOT...
...THE VEEBLE!
WAAK!!
SNATCH!!

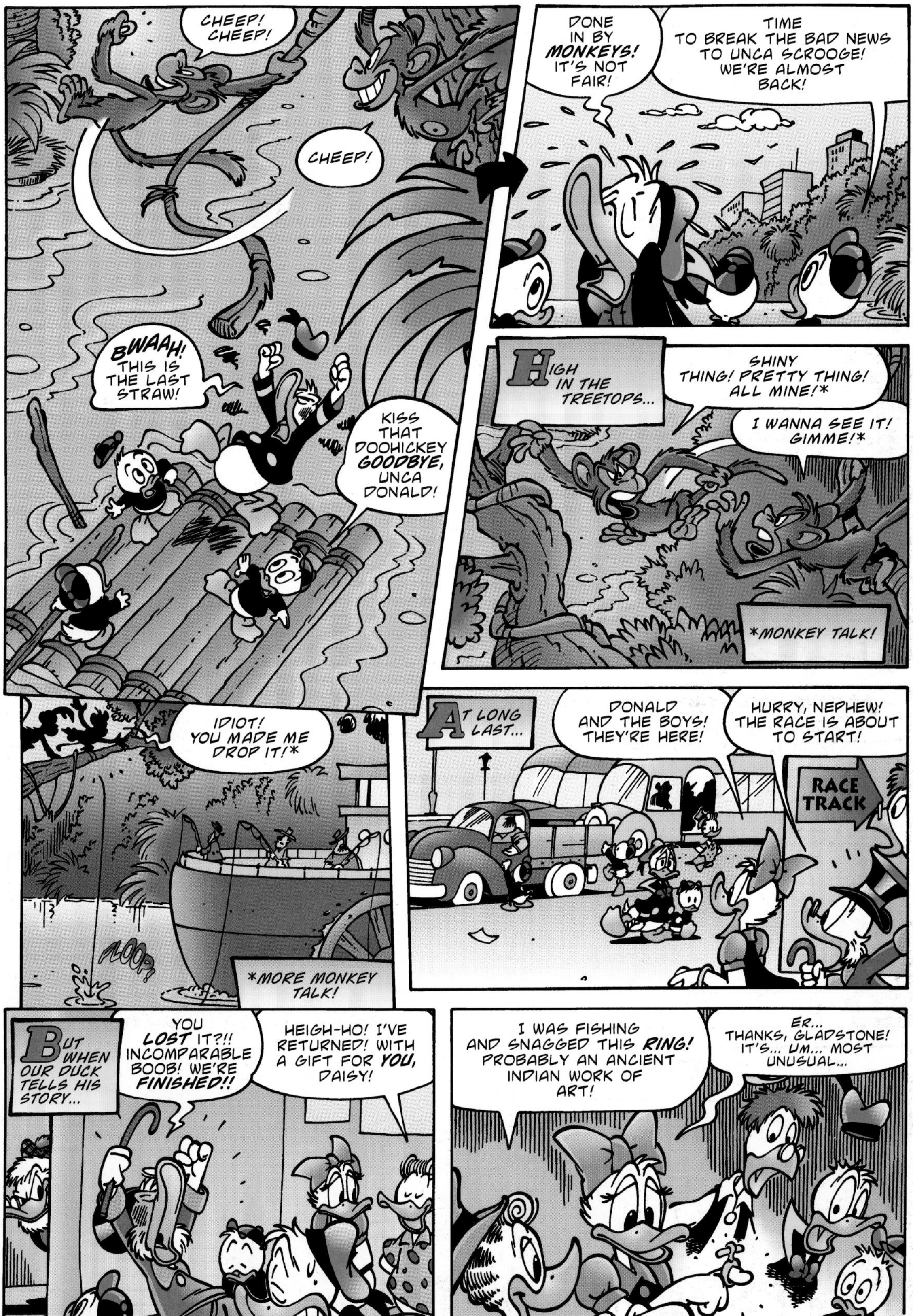
CHEEP! CHEEP!
CHEEP!
BWAAH! THIS IS THE LAST STRAW!
KISS THAT DOOHICKEY GOODBYE, UNCA DONALD!
DONE IN BY MONKEYS! IT'S NOT FAIR!
TIME TO BREAK THE BAD NEWS TO UNCA SCROOGE! WE'RE ALMOST BACK!
HIGH IN THE TREETOPS...
SHINY THING! PRETTY THING! ALL MINE!*
I WANNA SEE IT! GIMME!*
*MONKEY TALK!
IDIOT! YOU MADE ME DROP IT!*
PLOOP!
*MORE MONKEY TALK!
AT LONG LAST...
DONALD AND THE BOYS! THEY'RE HERE!
HURRY, NEPHEW! THE RACE IS ABOUT TO START!
RACE TRACK
BUT WHEN OUR DUCK TELLS HIS STORY...
YOU LOST IT?!! INCOMPARABLE BOOB! WE'RE FINISHED!!
HEIGH-HO! I'VE RETURNED! WITH A GIFT FOR YOU, DAISY!
I WAS FISHING AND SNAGGED THIS RING! PROBABLY AN ANCIENT INDIAN WORK OF ART!
ER... THANKS, GLADSTONE! IT'S... UM... MOST UNUSUAL...

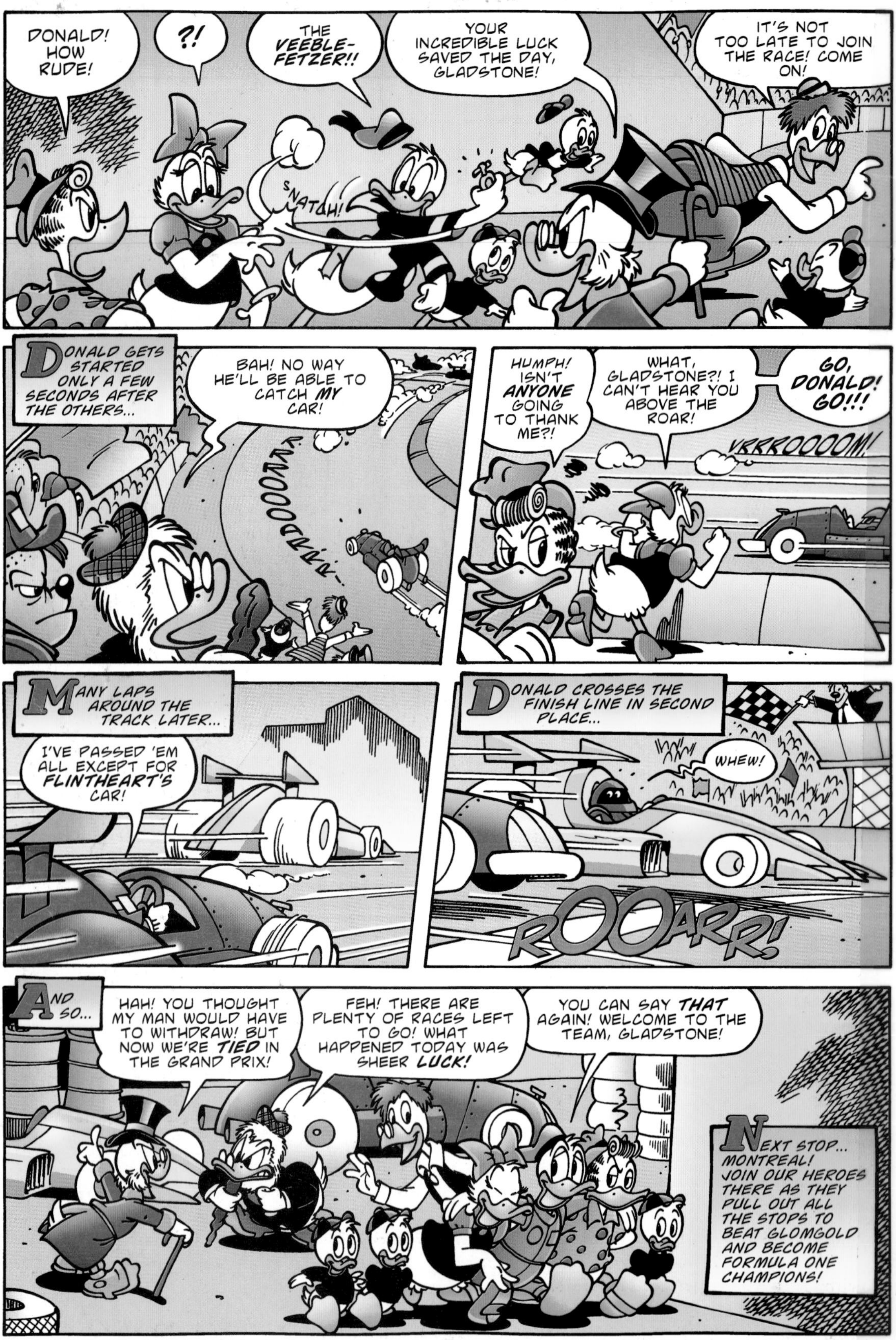
DONALD! HOW RUDE!
?!
THE VEEBLE-FETZER!!
SNATCH!
YOUR INCREDIBLE LUCK SAVED THE DAY, GLADSTONE!
IT'S NOT TOO LATE TO JOIN THE RACE! COME ON!
DONALD GETS STARTED ONLY A FEW SECONDS AFTER THE OTHERS...
BAH! NO WAY HE'LL BE ABLE TO CATCH MY CAR!
RRROOOOAAR!
HUMPH! ISN'T ANYONE GOING TO THANK ME?!
WHAT, GLADSTONE?! I CAN'T HEAR YOU ABOVE THE ROAR!
GO, DONALD! GO!!!
VRRROOOOOM!
MANY LAPS AROUND THE TRACK LATER...
I'VE PASSED 'EM ALL EXCEPT FOR FLINTHEART'S CAR!
DONALD CROSSES THE FINISH LINE IN SECOND PLACE...
WHEW!
ROOARR!
AND SO...
HAH! YOU THOUGHT MY MAN WOULD HAVE TO WITHDRAW! BUT NOW WE'RE TIED IN THE GRAND PRIX!
FEH! THERE ARE PLENTY OF RACES LEFT TO GO! WHAT HAPPENED TODAY WAS SHEER LUCK!
YOU CAN SAY THAT AGAIN! WELCOME TO THE TEAM, GLADSTONE!
NEXT STOP... MONTREAL! JOIN OUR HEROES THERE AS THEY PULL OUT ALL THE STOPS TO BEAT GLOMGOLD AND BECOME FORMULA ONE CHAMPIONS!